ESCAPE FROM
THE HOLOCAUST

The Do-It-Yourself
Jewish Adventure series

THE CARDINAL'S SNUFFBOX
by Kenneth Roseman

THE MELTING POT:
An Adventure in New York
by Kenneth Roseman

ESCAPE FROM THE HOLOCAUST
by Kenneth Roseman

ESCAPE FROM THE HOLOCAUST

KENNETH ROSEMAN

◆ ◆ ◆

Union of American Hebrew Congregations
New York

Library of Congress Cataloging in Publication Data

Roseman, Kenneth.
  Escape from the Holocaust.

  (The Do-It-Yourself Jewish Adventure series)
  Summary: As a young Jewish medical student in
Berlin in the 1930s, the reader is confronted with
choices that could mean the difference between freedom
and slavery, life and death.
  1. Holocaust, Jewish (1939–1945)—Juvenile fiction.
2. World War, 1939–1945—Jews—Rescue—Juvenile
fiction. 3. Plot-your-own stories. [1. Holocaust,
Jewish (1939–1945)—Fiction. 2. World War, 1939–
1945—Jews—Rescue—Fiction. 3. Plot-your-own
stories.] I. Title. II. Series.
PZ7.R71863Es 1985   [Fic]   85-8605
ISBN 0-8074-0307-5

Maps by Dyno Lowenstein

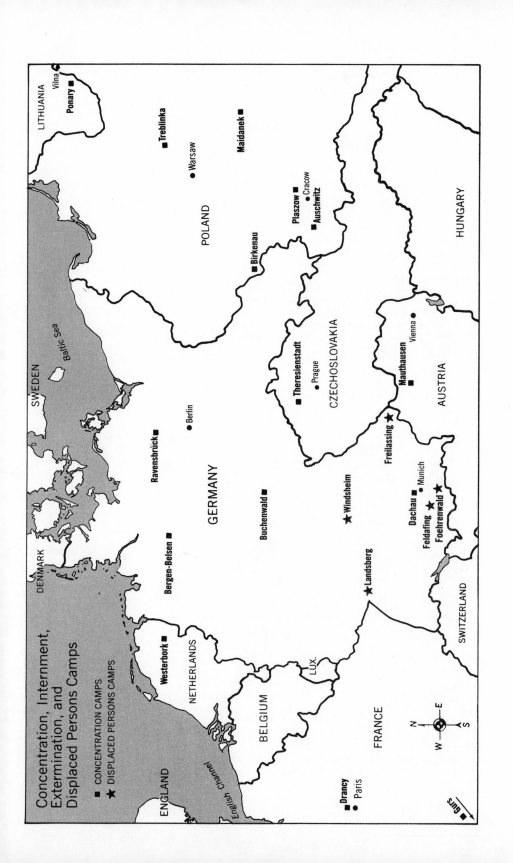

Concentration, Internment, Extermination, and Displaced Persons Camps

■ CONCENTRATION CAMPS
★ DISPLACED PERSONS CAMPS

ENGLAND

English Channel

Drancy ■
● Paris

FRANCE

N
W — E
S

Burg ■

NETHERLANDS

Westerbork ■

BELGIUM

LUX.

Bergen-Belsen ■

★ **Landsberg**

SWITZERLAND

DENMARK

GERMANY

Buchenwald ■

★ **Windsheim**

Dachau ■
Feldafing ★ ● Munich
Foehrenwald ★

★ **Freilassing**

Baltic Sea

SWEDEN

● Berlin

Ravensbrück ■

Theresienstadt ■
● Prague

CZECHOSLOVAKIA

Mauthausen ■

AUSTRIA

● Vienna

HUNGARY

Vilna ■
Ponary ■

LITHUANIA

Treblinka ■

● Warsaw

Maidanek ■

POLAND

Birkenau ■

Plaszow ■
● Cracow
Auschwitz ■

Europe — World War II

ATLANTIC
OCEAN

IRELAND

Cork

IRISH
SEA

ENGLAND

York

Great Yarmouth

London

Dover

English Channel

Le Havre

Caen

NORTH SEA

DENM

NETHERLANDS

Amsterdam
The Hague
Rotterdam

BELGIUM

Calais

LUX.

GERM

Paris

FRANCE

Strasbourg

Black F

Bay of
Biscay

Vichy

Zurich

SWITZ

Montreux

Geneva

Lyon

Bordeaux

Bergerac

Avignon

Marseilles

Lourdes

Corsica (France)

PORTUGAL

SPAIN

Madrid

Lisbon

MEDITERRANEAN SEA

NOR

ESCAPE FROM
THE HOLOCAUST

1

Y ou are about to read a very different kind of book. With most books you start on page 1 and continue straight through until the end. In *Escape from the Holocaust,* you'll proceed differently. Read the first five pages. At the bottom of page 5, you will find instructions telling you to make a choice before going ahead. Each choice leads you to different pages and to different experiences. In fact, you are the real creator of the story because you are the person making the choices.

The careful reader will notice that liberties were taken with the exact lapse of time between certain events. Moreover, not everything in this book happened in the life of one person. That would be impossible. But all the events are true; they all occurred in the lives of Jews who lived in Europe during the 1930s and 1940s, during and after those years we call the Holocaust or, in Hebrew, the "Sho'ah."

You may already know that the Nazis (National Socialists) ruled Germany from 1933–1945. During that time, Adolf Hitler and his armies set out to make Europe free of Jews ("judenrein") and of such other "undesirables" as Gypsies, the mentally retarded, journalists who wrote against Nazi policies, criminals, political opponents, Christians who resisted Nazism, and many others. By killing over 11,000,000 people, of whom about 6,000,000 were Jews, the Nazis almost achieved their goal, at least in the countries they had conquered.

But some European Jews did survive, and this book is about them—how they managed to live through the terror of those times and how they tried to reconstruct their lives. Reading this book may give you a sense of excitement, of adventure, and of triumph—because Jews and Judaism are still alive, despite Hitler's awful effort to rid the world of the Jewish people.

2

Be careful! Good feelings such as these can be misleading. They may blind you to some very painful and bitter truths. As you read, remember that, for every Jew who survived, three were killed; for every Jew who was liberated from the concentration camps, seventy-five perished in brutal deaths. Never forget the terrible price that was exacted from the Jewish people during those years. Even though this book may help you learn about a terrible time in human history in an enjoyable way, never think of the Holocaust as a game.

And never forget that survival was difficult, dangerous, and unpredictable. To survive, one needed help, stamina, courage, will, and a great deal of luck. To survive, one had to endure more than most people can even imagine. If you have ever been frightened, remember that your fright was very small compared to the daily fear and terror of Jews in Nazi Europe. If you have ever been hungry, remember that your hunger stopped with your next meal while theirs continued for days, weeks, months, and even years. And, if you have ever been lonely, remember how much worse it must have been to know that every other member of your family and all your friends were gone, probably dead. They had disappeared into the mysterious and terrifying concentration camps, and you were totally, sadly, and darkly alone.

To know and to remember—that is what this book is about. Most of all, I hope you will discover that, if the evil power of the Nazis was real, so was the courage, goodness, determination, and faith of many other people. And, if human beings could create the Holocaust and its terror, human beings (you and I, all of us) also have the power to prevent another Holocaust and to create a society where goodness, caring, and love rule human affairs. As you find words in italics, look them up in the glossary at the back.

Now, turn to page 3.

3

Berlin is a beautiful, glorious city. Tall, leafy trees line wide avenues, and elegant men and women stroll along the boulevards. Every evening, you can hear fine music and attend the best theaters. The University of Berlin is considered by many the best in the world!

It's the university that brought you to Berlin two years ago. You remember clearly the conversations you had with your parents in Cracow, trying to persuade them that a young Jew had little or no chance to become a doctor in Poland. You would not even be permitted to enroll at the university in Poland. But, in Germany, you could attend classes with other students and study medicine with the finest professors. Finally, they let you go, but only on condition that you live with a Jewish family and attend synagogue every *Shabbat* morning. You had no difficulty accepting those conditions, and you've had no regrets since coming to Berlin. Your studies have gone well; your life has been a whirl of excitement. You have made a good choice. First, you will attend the university; then, if you score well on the examination, you will be admitted to medical school; finally, you will fulfill your dream of becoming a doctor.

4

There is another side of Berlin, a side of the city you don't often like to think about. The worldwide *Depression* has left tens of thousands of people without work—homeless and hungry. These people live in alleys or in shacks of scrap lumber; they never have enough to eat; they are cold in winter and hot in summer; and they are always angry, especially when they see people like you, people who are able to study at the university and walk along the spacious avenues in handsome clothing.

In their bitterness, these people have begun to follow a new political leader, Adolf Hitler. Hitler has promised that he will improve their lives and restore their sense of dignity. He has told them that they are not to blame for their sad situation, that they have been victims of an international Jewish conspiracy. Jews caused their misfortunes, he says, and they believe him, even though the Jews of Germany are suffering from the *Depression* just as much as their neighbors. His solution is to get rid of the Jews. Once that happens, he claims, things will get better.

The voters of Germany agree, for they cast their ballots for Herr Hitler in the election of 1933, and he is named chancellor, the German equivalent of prime minister. Germany is wild with expectations for better days, but you are afraid. Is it really possible that he will carry out his plans or were those just promises he made to win votes?

5

You do not have to wait long for your answer. Within months, Hitler's program begins to take effect. Signs are posted on Jewish businesses, telling other Germans not to buy in those stores. Jews are fired from their jobs, especially in the schools and the government. Non-Jewish friends no longer come to your home, and they even turn their heads aside when they pass you in the street. From time-to-time, you hear of attacks made on Jews: old men pulled into the street from their shops and forced to scrub the gutters, people beaten by the *Brownshirts,* even occasional murders. A cloud of fear descends upon the Jewish community in Berlin and throughout Germany.

Yet your studies at the university have been going very well. You don't want to give them up; it's very important to you to become a doctor and to return to Poland to work in the Jewish communities there. Perhaps this outbreak of anti-Semitism is just temporary; maybe it will pass. After all, this is a country of civilization, the land of Bach and Beethoven. People will not stand for such attacks on German citizens for much longer.

On the other hand, perhaps Chancellor Hitler is really serious about making Germany free of Jews. Could it be that these attacks are just the beginning of the actual destruction of Germany's Jews?

If you believe the outbreak of anti-Semitism is only temporary, and you decide to stay in Germany to complete your studies, turn to page 6.

If you decide to sacrifice a medical education for your own safety and return to Cracow, turn to page 7.

6

Jewish professors have been dismissed from their posts at the university, but students have been allowed to remain. You have never been reluctant to identify yourself as a Jew, but you try to hide your Polish past. Eastern European Jews are being expelled from the *Third Reich* as quickly as possible.

Just before your graduation, you are called into the school's office and told that you will not be allowed to finish. "No Jews may become doctors," you are told. "We cannot permit non-*Aryan* inferiors to treat Germans." You are heartbroken—all those years of serious, hard study now amount to nothing.

As you leave the building, a leading member of the Jewish community meets you on the street. "I know what just happened," he says. "It's a terrible injustice. But I hope you will stay with us, here in Berlin. We need you. So many Jews are being hurt by the *SA* that we need medical help—and no non-Jewish doctors will treat us anymore. Although you are not yet a doctor, you could be of real help."

If you choose to remain in Berlin,
turn to page 9.

If you think that there is really no future for
Jews in Germany, and you decide to leave,
turn to page 10.

7

It's good to be back in Cracow with your family although you cannot continue your medical studies at the university there. In Poland, Jews are not permitted to attend classes. You arrange to work with an elderly doctor, learning what you can as his apprentice.

In September 1939, the Germans invade Poland and, within three weeks, the country surrenders. Anti-Jewish actions begin almost immediately. Laws are passed stating what Jews may do and what they may not do, where Jews may live and where they may not live. Soon, Jews from the countryside are forced to move into the Jewish area in the city of Cracow; it's the beginning of a policy of collecting all Polish Jews into small districts called ghettos. Because of the overcrowding, there is not enough food or space; it seems that the Germans are pursuing their policy of securing "Lebensraum," room to live, at your expense.

The Jewish community tries to maintain its schools, cultural events, religious activities—those things that Jewish people treasure most—but it becomes increasingly difficult. The Germans apply more pressure every day. Finally, you see *the handwriting on the wall;* their intention is to destroy the future of Jewish life in Poland.

If you flee north to Vilna in Lithuania,
turn to page 11.

If you choose to stay in Cracow because
leaving your family again is unbearable,
turn to page 12.

If you decide to escape south to Budapest,
turn to page 13.

8

The idea of taking a ship to Cuba, without any guarantee that you will be able to go ashore, scares you as does the notion of illegally stowing away on an Ireland-bound vessel. Instead, you take the overnight train from the Friedrichstrasse station to the city of Essen and then hide aboard a train headed for Amsterdam. As you enter this old city, you are struck by its beauty.

Your medical training in Germany helps you get a job as an attendant at the Burgerweeshuis, the city orphanage. You find a small boarding house, facing the Ouda Schans Canal, where you rent a room and take your meals for a very reasonable rate. You settle into a stable life and make friends in a *Zionist* youth group. All goes well until. . . .

. . . Until May 10, 1940, when the "Blitzkrieg," lightning-fast war, begins. Led by tank divisions, the German army overruns the Netherlands. Four days later, the country surrenders and is occupied by the Germans. Most of the people are bitterly unhappy, but some join the Dutch Nazi party to help the Germans. You are more afraid of them than of the Germans themselves, and you wonder what to do. Urged by some friends in the *Zionist* groups, you can go into hiding; you can leave for England like some Dutch Jews, though it is extremely dangerous; or you can flee south to France.

If you choose to go into hiding,
turn to page 14.

If you risk crossing the English Channel,
turn to page 15.

If you decide to flee to France,
turn to page 16.

9

Your studies mean so much to you that they nearly blind you to what is happening in the streets of Berlin. Everyday, you hear of beatings and murders. You even saw a *Chasid* being dragged through the streets by his beard.

"But those are Eastern European Jews," you try to persuade yourself. "They're not like me. Here, in this cradle of western civilization, here in this land of fine music, art, and culture, here no one would attack me. I'm more like the Germans now than I am like those foreigners."

You are listening to the radio on November 9, 1938, when you hear that a Jewish young man, upset because his parents had been arrested in Poland, had shot and killed an official of the German Embassy in Paris. Suddenly, the streets are filled with gangsters wearing *Brownshirt* uniforms. It is clear that the government has let them loose to destroy the Jewish community. Books are thrown out into the street and burned; stores are looted and destroyed; people are humiliated, hurt, even killed. From your window, you can see a crowd ripping up a Torah and laughing as the pieces float down the sewer.

"Kristallnacht," the night of broken glass, convinces you that you have made a mistake. Now, you must take action.

If you try to leave Germany,
turn to page 19.

If you think leaving will be impossible and
try to hide in Berlin,
turn to page 20.

10

The Nazis seem to prefer forcing Jews out of the country. Obtaining an exit permit requires standing in long lines, day-after-day, and agreeing to give almost all your possessions and money to the government. You are left with little.

You travel to Hamburg, Germany's main port city. There are two ships in the port. You must decide which to take. The Saint Louis, a large passenger ship from the Hamburg-America Line, has agreed to take 900 Jews to Cuba; you can bribe one of the officials to give you an entry visa to that island. The other ship is a small freighter going to Ireland.

Your decision will be difficult. Visas to Cuba look correct, but who knows whether or not they will be honored. Perhaps you won't be permitted to enter the country after all. That's a risk. On the other hand, the freighter is not supposed to carry passengers. You'll have to get aboard illegally and stay hidden as the ship crosses the North Sea and makes its way to Cork. There is, of course, always the possibility of trying a land route.

If you select the Saint Louis,
turn to page 17.

If you risk stowing away on the freighter,
turn to page 18.

If you decide to go by land to Holland and
take your chances there,
turn to page 8.

If you decide to try an optional southern land
route, through Trieste,
turn to page 93.

11

Vilna, the "Jerusalem of the North," the city of the great *Elijah Gaon,* a place of great Jewish culture and activity, is stimulated by the hustle-bustle and competition among various Jewish groups: *Zionists, Bundists,* Orthodox Jews, and *Haskalniks.* Walking in the street, you can hear discussions of a variety of Jewish ideas. That the Germans and the Russians signed a friendship pact in 1939 affects little. It's quiet on the surface, but underneath there is always a current of anti-Semitism and the Russian threat that "undesirables" will be sent to Siberian labor camps.

In 1941, despite a peace treaty, the Nazis treacherously attack Russia and overrun Lithuania. You are now in the same situation you were in two years ago in Cracow: You are required to wear a yellow Star of David and to endure anti-Jewish laws and persecution. Your greatest fear is that you will be among the nearly 500 Jews deported every day to the concentration camp at Ponary. Yet life goes on. You and the other Jews resist by trying to keep Jewish life alive. Some belong to Kibbutz Akiva, training to go to Palestine.

On *Yom Kippur* 1941, 1,700 Jews are arrested as they come out of the synagogues and are sent to their death at Ponary. Thousands of Jews protest. The Germans break up the demonstration viciously, killing many people. At least Jews have openly expressed their opposition. Perhaps now the world will take notice and help.

If you decide to flee from Vilna,
turn to page 21.

If you decide to join a partisan unit in the
region of Vilna,
turn to page 22.

12

You left your family once to study in Germany. Now realizing how precious they are to you, leaving them a second time is an option you will not consider. You are going to stay with them in Cracow, no matter what happens.

As the Germans take tighter control over the ghetto, conditions worsen. Business activity is suspended in the summer of 1942. Food rations are cut in half. The Germans round up many of the residents and as many children as they can catch in a violent *Aktion,* herding them into a large square near the railroad station. There, they tell them that, because of the shortage of food, they are being resettled in the countryside on farms where they can work, have enough to eat, and live safely. Later, a Jewish courier sneaks into the ghetto and informs the *Judenrat* that all those people were taken to Maidanek Concentration Camp and massacred. It's almost too much to believe, but it is true. You've heard of killings at a ravine called Babi Yar near Kiev and the harsh treatment of the Jews in the Warsaw Ghetto. Why should Cracow be any different?

Your family insists that you try to escape, but you continue to resist. Family is all you have left. You will not abandon your parents, brothers, and sisters.

If you decide to stay with your family,
turn to page 23.

If you are finally persuaded to try to get
away from Cracow,
turn to page 24.

13

Budapest, Hungary's capital, is a beautiful city, split into two sections by the wide Danube River or Duna, as it is known here. Even during the war, one can still hear good music and eat fine food. During most of the war, the Germans have been content to station a modest occupation force in Hungary, leaving the day-to-day responsibilities of government in the hands of Admiral Miklos Horthy. Horthy's job is to do what the Nazis tell him to do, but he is also a patriotic Hungarian who fiercely dislikes the German invaders.

One way he demonstrates his resistance to the Germans is by delaying the deportation of Jewish Hungarians to the death camps. While Horthy takes as long as possible to act on Nazi orders, thousands of Jews are able to flee to Russia, where they will be safe during the war.

Eventually, the Germans take a more direct hand in the deportations. On March 19, 1944, they begin to round up Hungarian Jews and ship them to Auschwitz. You've experienced *Aktions* before, and you know that it means the end of Hungarian Jewry. If you remain in Budapest, it won't be long before you are caught and sent to the gas chamber. You must get out of the city. However, it has become far more difficult with the German army in direct control.

If you choose to get help from foreign diplomats,
turn to page 25.

If you decide to ask the Judenrat for assistance,
turn to page 26.

14

You and four other young people turn to a non-Jewish neighbor, Mr. Drent, whose house on Prinsengracht has a small attic room. The Drents have always been extremely friendly to Jewish people, and you have heard them express their dislike of the Germans. You ask if you and your friends can hide in the attic, at least for a few weeks until you can make other plans. You feel bad asking them to take such a risk, but you have no alternative. To your great relief, they agree, telling you: "Anything we can do to save our neighbors from the hated Nazis is our patriotic duty."

The attic is cramped, with barely enough room for the five of you to sleep. A bookcase conceals the door and is moved aside only late at night so that you can empty the chamberpot, receive provisions for the next day, and stretch a little. You spend most of your time reading and talking with each other in whispers. No sound and no light must escape from your self-imposed prison, lest someone discover your hiding place.

The few weeks of your refuge stretch into eighteen months, but the Drent family and their friends, the Van Dyks, won't hear of any change. "Don't worry," they tell you. "We Dutch will always stand by you." However, one night, Storm Troopers dash through the house, looking for your hiding place; you must have been betrayed by a collaborator.

If they find your secret refuge,
turn to page 27.

If you remain undiscovered,
turn to page 28.

15

To leave the Netherlands will not be easy. German soldiers guard all of the seaports. Aware that many people will try to cross the English Channel by boat, they are especially vigilant in the southern part of the country, the section where the Channel is narrowest.

But the Dutch have lived with the sea for a long time. Truss Wijsmuller introduces you to a Mr. Klaas who reassures you. "Meet me tomorrow morning; you're going on a picnic in the country." And so you do—to the small town of Den Helder, north of Amsterdam. As you sit on the beach there, eating bread and cheese, you are joined by a broad-shouldered young man. Mr. Klaas introduces you to his brother, Henryk, and they ask you to follow them. Hidden in a small cove is a fishing boat, already loaded with nine other Jewish refugees. You will complete the *minyan.* Of course, you must wait until nightfall before attempting the crossing.

Because Henryk Klaas is an expert seaman, the German patrol boats do not spot you. You land at Great Yarmouth and are met by Lola Hann Warburg, one of the founders of *Youth Aliyah.* She suggests you join a group of Jewish young people outside the northern city of York. They are learning the techniques of farming so they can eventually move to Palestine. You join the group. After the war, however, unable to locate your parents, you decide to join a cousin who lives in Canada.

Turn to page 29.

16

Getting from Holland into France will not be easy. You must travel 400 miles through Belgium. The entire region is crawling with German soldiers. One false move, and you will end up in front of a firing squad.

You decide that the best route would be along one of the country's famous canals. The banks are covered with bushes, and you can always duck under water, breathing through a tube if necessary. This route is longer, but it seems safer.

Halfway from Amsterdam to the Belgian border, you must cross three, heavily guarded, wide rivers. You slip across the Rhine and the Waal without any difficulty, but the guards on the banks of the Maas spot you and start shooting. Luckily for you, a canal boat passes, and you are able to swim to the other shore. You continue along the Willems Canal and then follow the Meuse River into France. When you finally get to the famous World War I battlefield of Château Thierry, you stop and think.

Paris is not very far away. Perhaps you would be safer in a large city. But the Germans have concentrated their forces in northern France and might arrest you in Paris. If you continue on to the south of France, you might stand less chance of being caught.

If you decide to hide in Paris,
turn to page 31.

If you choose to go to southern France,
turn to page 32.

17

The Atlantic crossing is uneventful, and you feel hopeful. As the anchor drops into the water in Havana harbor, you are sure that a good, new life awaits you. The ship's officers go ashore. It is a long time before they return, and the longer they meet with the Cuban authorities, the more concerned you become. All your papers are in order. What could be going wrong?

When the ship's captain returns, he announces that there is a problem with the visas; the Cubans refuse to honor the entry permits. He will try to change their minds, and officials from various Jewish organizations are attempting to secure refuge for you, whether in Cuba, Panama, the United States, or some other country.

It is so hot and crowded on the ship that people become ill. Sailors with rifles prevent you from jumping over the side and swimming to shore. Everyone is anxious and angry. Finally, after an entire month of delay, the captain reports that no country is willing to accept you. The ship will return to Europe, where people will be put ashore at several ports.

You realize what this means: Hitler is free to do whatever he wants to the Jews; no country cares enough to protect you from him.

When the ship nears Europe, you must decide where to disembark.

If you go ashore at Le Havre in France, turn to page 33.

If you prefer Rotterdam in Holland, turn to page 34.

18

At a restaurant, some sailors talk about their ship which is sailing that night for Ireland. You slip down to the docks and sneak aboard during the confusion of the departure. You hide in a lifeboat. But, during a safety drill at sea, you are discovered and taken to the captain's cabin.

You decide to tell him the truth: You are Jewish and fleeing the anti-Semitism of the Nazis. He dismisses the sailor who is guarding you and closes the door. "Listen," he tells you, "I am a member of the Reformed Church. What Hitler is doing in Germany is against everything I believe in as a Christian. I will protect you and let you off the ship at the first safe port." You can hardly believe your ears, and you thank him warmly.

At the Irish port of Cork, you go ashore and then find your way across the Irish Sea to England. The immigration authorities there give you a choice.

Either you can apply for British citizenship and join the Royal Air Force or receive a temporary transit visa and seek to go to the United States.

If you join the RAF,
turn to page 35.

If you try to continue on to America,
turn to page 36.

19

Getting out of Germany is increasingly difficult. After "Kristallnacht," the Nazis have put more guards on the borders, especially those with Holland, Belgium, France, and Switzerland. But an even greater problem exists. The other countries of western Europe and the Americas do not want to accept a flood of Jewish refugees—even a small flood. It is hard to get out of Germany, but it is even more difficult to get into any other country, especially one where you might be safe.

Your life is turned upside-down. Everything you had counted on is no longer possible. You can't sleep, both for fear of being arrested and thrown into the concentration camp at Buchenwald and because you are trying to figure out what you must do to save your life.

Distraught, you can come up with only two ideas: You can appeal for help to some German friends you knew at the university, or, doubtful as to whom you can trust, you can flee from Germany. A southern route toward Vienna and Budapest seems safest to you.

If you decide to appeal to friends,
turn to page 37.

If you choose to flee south,
turn to page 38.

20

During the anti-Semitic outburst of "Kristallnacht," the night of broken glass, and for the next several days, you stay sensibly hidden. When you do emerge from your shelter, you find that the *SA* thugs have destroyed the Jewish community. Synagogues have been burned and looted; holy books, Torahs, mezuzahs, and other ritual objects lie in the gutter; Jews, many of whom believed that this could never happen, are devastated by the tragedy and confused about what to do next.

You feel alone, abandoned, wishing someone would take you by the hand and lead you to safety. But then a fragment of a saying from *Pirke Avot* crosses your mind: "If I am not for myself, who will be for me?" You've never fully understood this saying before, but now you do; you've got to save yourself; you are responsible for taking whatever action is needed to stay alive. No one else will do that for you.

You are convinced that you will die if you remain in Germany. Denmark seems the safest and nearest country to which to flee.

If you choose to seek safety in Denmark,
turn to page 39.

If you think that it will be too dangerous to
flee, and you are better off trying to hide in
Berlin,
turn to page 40.

21

As the Nazis make Jewish life in Vilna more and more unbearable, you feel that you have made the correct decision in choosing to flee from the city. Where to go, however, is not an easy matter, especially now that the German army controls all of Europe west and south of Lithuania.

On *Shabbat* afternoon between *Minchah* and *Ma'ariv,* you are studying with the other people in the synagogue. As you rhythmically recite the lines of the *Gemara,* a thought comes to you. Generations of Jews, when they were confused or had a question, sought the advice of their rabbi. You will do the same.

After *Havdalah,* you knock on the door of the Amshenover *Rebbe*'s home. Rabbi Shimon Kalisch is a well-respected religious leader; he will be able to tell you what to do.

When Rabbi Kalisch informs you that he, too, is prepared to leave, you are further convinced that this is the right course. The rabbi tells you that he has been able to secure several transit visas to travel through Russia and Japan on the way to Curaçao. You don't even know where Curaçao is, but he tells you that it is one of the few places that does not require an entry visa and is, therefore, still open to refugee Jews. The Japanese consul, Senpo Sugihara, violated instructions by issuing the visas, but they are perfectly legal.

Rabbi Kalisch invites you to go with him, and you accept. You gather up your few belongings and meet him and his family at the train station the next morning.

Turn to page 41.

22

At four o'clock in the morning, you assemble with others at the bathhouse on Straszuna Street for the work assigned to you by the ghetto authorities. You march away as if you were headed for your work, but, when you reach Konske Street, you dash out the side gate of the ghetto. Quickly, you rip the yellow Star of David from your coat and run as fast as you can, knowing that the Germans will not be far behind.

Outside the city, it is easier to hide, but German patrols are criss-crossing the region, looking for you and others like you, with the aid of bloodhounds. However, you are able to elude them by sprinkling pepper and paprika on the trail. The dogs' sense of smell fails when they sniff these strong spices.

After two weeks of sleeping under bushes and stealing food, you stumble upon a partisan camp. You approach the partisans with your hands up, afraid they might mistake you for a German. When you explain what has happened to you, the partisans believe your story and accept you. They offer you the chance to join one of two Jewish units, the 106th Division or a group called "The Vengeance."

If you select the 106th Division,
turn to page 42.

If you choose the unit called "The Vengeance,"
turn to page 43.

23

In the spring of 1943, all of you are arrested and deported to the labor camp at Plaszow, where you are required to work twelve hours a day to make clothing for the German army. Others slave in the limestone quarries; you are glad that you are, at least, spared that horror. To be assigned to the quarries is to be condemned to death.

The guards, some of the worst human beings imaginable, criminals and maniacs, take pleasure in whipping and torturing the prisoners for no apparent reason. Hunting Jews is their recreation. Some of them let vicious dogs attack inmates and laugh while the animals tear the men and women to pieces. Amon Gett, the camp commander, rides through the camp on a white horse, picking out people for execution as casually as if he were selecting fruit in a market. One day, he shot your father and eleven other men just for target practice—and you had to stand at attention and watch.

Although making clothing for the army is, of course, better than working in a quarry, conditions at Plaszow are still awful. You don't know how much more brutality you can witness without going mad. Escape seems the only possible solution. Then, you weigh the personal dangers you would face if you tried to escape. You also realize that escape means that Amon Gett will take brutal revenge on those who remain behind. You cannot take that responsibility. Yet you must consider your alternatives and make a decision.

If you decide to escape from Plaszow,
turn to page 44.

If you choose to stay in the camp,
turn to page 45.

24

Escape from the ghetto of Cracow will not be easy. The Germans have posted guards all around the Jewish area and have threatened the police of the *Judenrat* with immediate execution if Jews are allowed to escape. "But," you think to yourself, "if the Germans are going to kill me anyway, I have an obligation to myself to try to escape. I want to live."

During an *Aktion,* you hide in a room, concealed behind a stove. When the Jewish police search the house, they pass by your hiding place; after all, who would want to move a red-hot stove? As they leave, you breathe deeply. For the moment, at least, you are safe. Getting out of the ghetto, however, will still require a great deal of luck.

Some people have managed to escape by crawling through underground sewer pipes. This appears to be the sole way to get out alive since the only people who leave the ghetto legally are those who, having died of disease or starvation, are carried out on carts and buried in the old Jewish cemetery. Remembering this gives you an idea.

If you decide to escape through the sewer pipes, turn to page 46.

If you choose to escape by some original plan, turn to page 47.

25

You cross the Duna River by way of the Erzsebet-Hid Bridge and enter the old, inner city of Pest. There, where most of the diplomatic and government buildings are located, you head for the Swedish Embassy. Rumors have circulated that a young Swedish diplomat named Raoul Wallenberg has ways of helping Jews. You must find him.

Wallenberg is, in fact, not hard to locate. You ask for him at the front desk of the embassy and are directed into a room with other Jews, sitting on benches, awaiting interviews. When you are ushered into Wallenberg's office, he tells you that he will give you Swedish citizenship. With the proper documents, you will be considered a citizen of a neutral country, unlikely to be bothered by the Germans. Just in case, however, he also has a safe place called the "House of Glass," an old factory on Vadasz Street, where you can stay until Hungary is liberated or you can leave the country.

Apparently, Wallenberg has made similar arrangements for many Jews, and you feel very confident as he signs, stamps, and seals the papers. Then, however, you stop to think. The Germans are not stupid. They probably know that this is just a trick for your protection, which they will not accept.

If you doubt that Wallenberg's papers will protect you, and you decide to strike out on your own,
turn to page 48.

If you choose to go through with the Swedish arrangement,
turn to page 49.

26

You walk along a wide boulevard. Turning left onto a smaller street, you stand before the Great Synagogue of Pest, topped by two towers with onion-shaped domes. Next to it stands the Jewish community building with its beautiful, pillared arcade. It is in this annex that the *Judenrat,* headed by Rudolf Kastner, meets. Kastner has a reputation for helping Jews escape from the Nazis. The story is told that he even traded money and trucks to get some Jews out of the concentration camp at Bergen-Belsen. In many other cities, the members of the *Judenrat* have used their power and position to save themselves and their families, disregarding the needs of the community. That does not seem to be the case in Budapest.

You stand in a long line, awaiting your turn for an interview. When Kastner finally sees you, you learn that the stories about him are true. He offers you two possible ways to save yourself: sneaking out of the city and getting to Russia where you would be much safer or traveling across Hungary and hiding with a Christian family, disguised as a relative.

If you choose to leave Budapest for Russia,
turn to page 50.

If you decide to travel across Hungary, facing
the danger of German military occupiers, and
hide with a Christian family,
turn to page 51.

27

The Storm Troopers pull you from the attic and drag you down the stairs. To your horror, Mr. and Mrs. Van Dyk are shoved up against the wall and shot. You pray that the Drents escaped. "That's what happens to people who oppose the triumph of the *Third Reich,*" the soldiers scream at you. Then, you are marched off to Waterlooplein where, with other Jews, you are placed on a bus and shipped to the transit camp at Westerbork. There the conditions are bad; the fear, uncertainty, and frightening rumors are worse.

Every day, some inmates are selected and put on trains out of the camp. They are never heard from again; you can only imagine the worst fate for them. Within a few days, you are selected for transport to the east. You and thousands of other Jews are marched up to the siding where a train of cattle cars stands. The weather is bitterly cold, and you have only a light jacket; the sides of the cars are a lattice-work of slats, open enough for the freezing wind to whip through the interior. You are crowded into the car so tightly that no one is able to sit. The door slides shut, and you hear the click of a lock. With such terrible weather, hunger, and pain from cramped conditions, it is no surprise that, when you look about in the morning, you find fifteen people dead, frozen in an upright position. You and the other, younger prisoners move them, stacking the corpses in one corner. You wonder how long you can hold out under these conditions.

If you think your only chance to survive is to escape from the train,
turn to page 52.

If you despair and remain on the train,
turn to page 53.

28

Safe for the present behind the little door and its concealing bookcase, you and your friends read every book you can
find and hold long, whispered conversations. To keep your
sanity while you are cooped up, you construct elaborate
plans for the future. Sometimes these plans depress you, but
fantasy seems the only way to keep your grip on reality.

One night, Mr. Drent opens the door to the hiding place
and warns you. There is a story circulating in town that
Heinrich Himmler, Hitler's second-in-command, had
planned a mass deportation of Dutch Jews, but his doctor,
Felix Kersten, a man Himmler trusts, has convinced him to
change those plans. Nonetheless, Mr. Drent is convinced
that a major hunt for hidden Jews is planned in the near
future. He thinks you had better make new arrangements
since some neighbors might already know about your exis-
tence in his house.

*If you decide to find a new hiding place
within Amsterdam,
turn to page 54.*

*If you think you ought to get out of the city
and take your chances in the countryside,
turn to page 55.*

29

Just before sailing for Canada, you learn that none of your family in Poland has survived the war; they all died in Auschwitz, most of them during the winter of 1943–1944. A deep sadness fills your soul; at unexpected moments you burst into tears. The only family left is your cousin in Canada.

After a sea voyage of twelve days, you leave the ship at Montreal and board the train for a three-day trip across this immense country to Winnepeg. Your arrival coincides with the first blizzard of the winter, and you wonder whether you have made a good decision. However, the outside cold is overcome by the warmth of the reception you receive, and you cry again—but this time in joy and excitement. As you sit with your newly-found family, you feel that a sense of life and purpose has been restored to you.

After a while, however, you are becoming restless. You feel that you must make a future for yourself. During long discussions with your cousin, you find that there are two possible paths you can follow: A land owner, your cousin's friend, offers you a job as manager of his wheat farm in the little town of Morden, Manitoba, just south of Winnepeg. You also learn that Toronto, an important city with opportunities for employment and a rich social and religious life, has a large community of Holocaust survivors.

If you decide to use your agricultural training on the wheat farm,
turn to page 145.

If you choose to try your luck in Toronto,
turn to page 142.

30

You're still in prison. You feel imaginary bars of iron pressing against you, a heavy weight on your heart. Being Jewish oppresses you. You have paid dearly for the privilege of being a Jew, losing your entire family, your career, almost your life; you think that enough is enough. It would have been so much easier if your grandparents had converted to Christianity!

You turn to a pastor of a Calvinist church and ask that he instruct you in Christianity. For a year, he teaches you once a week, telling you about Jesus, sin, and forgiveness. You are not sure that you believe in what he says, but, if that is what it takes to escape being Jewish, you are willing to agree. Finally, you are accepted as a convert, and you become a Christian.

The church helps you purchase a booth near the railroad station, where you sell newspapers, magazines, cigarettes, and other small items. You have certainly not become a success, but you are sure that your children will not have to suffer the same handicap that nearly cost you your life.

END

31

Living as a refugee in Paris would be difficult except that there are so many others like you. You band together and help each other. That makes survival possible. Still, living in the sewers and digging through garbage cans for food is degrading. You wonder whether you made the right choice. It's idle speculation, however, because you can't go back and start over again.

Paris is a gloomy city during the summer of 1942. On July 14, there is no celebration of Bastille Day; in fact, the Germans put on a parade of their own to demonstrate their power and superiority to the French people. Two days later, squads of German *SS* are sent through the city. Rumors reach you that they are rounding up all the Jews they can find and taking them to a central prison. You desperately think of a way to hide. The sewers may be the safest place for you. Perhaps you can outwit the Germans. On the other hand, the sewers can also be a trap. Perhaps it would be safer to hide in an unlikely place like a Catholic cemetery.

If you choose to stay in your familiar sewers,
turn to page 56.

If you decide to hide in the cemetery,
turn to page 57.

32

Roughly the southern half of France remains under French control—not independent French control, but a puppet government established by the Germans, existing only with their approval, located in the town of Vichy. As long as this government, headed by Pierre Laval, does what the Germans want, it will continue to exist; if its efforts, particularly to rid southern France of Jews, are not sufficiently enthusiastic, the government will disappear.

Nonetheless, it does seem safer for a Jew to live in Vichy than in those areas under direct German control. You meet a number of other Jewish refugees, and the relaxed attitude of the local authorities leads all of you to take a few chances. You speak in public places about matters of Jewish concern, and you even sing a few songs in *Yiddish* when you think no one is listening.

But Vichy is changing. A new and more anti-Semitic Commissioner for Jewish Affairs is appointed, and he begins a roundup of Jews, especially those who were not born in France. By the fall of 1942, large numbers of Jews have been put into the internment camp at Gurs.

If you are unlucky enough to be arrested,
turn to page 58.

If you are warned in time, however, and you
flee to the city of Marseilles,
turn to page 59.

33

When you leave the ship at Le Havre, you are surprised to find a representative of the Jewish community of Paris on the dock. You and the others who have decided to disembark in France are greeted warmly, given a good meal, and put aboard the train to France's capital city.

Once in Paris, you are housed in a dormitory with other young Jewish refugees. The Jewish community takes care of your needs, and they even find you a job, working as a nurse's helper in a hospital. You feel good; at least your medical training is being put to use helping other people. It's not the same as being a doctor, but, in your situation, something is better than nothing—and nothing is what you would have had in either Germany or Poland.

The newspapers are full of news of Nazi conquests. The Sudetenland of Czechoslovakia was virtually given to them when the British agreed not to object, and the invasion of your homeland, Poland, took only a few weeks. There are rumors that they will now turn west and attack the Low Countries and France. The French military command is certain that the forts along the defensive Maginot Line will prevent them from conquering the country, and you feel somewhat reassured.

The French are sadly mistaken. In a lightning-fast strike, German tanks race through Holland and Belgium; it takes barely a month for France to surrender. You are trapped in Paris, a city now administered by Nazis. You must leave your job and go into hiding.

Turn to page 31.

34

You leave the Saint Louis at the Dutch port city of Rotterdam. At first, you are terribly confused: You don't speak the language; you are not familiar with the city; you have no friends. You lean back against a trash container and wonder how you will be able to survive.

After what seems like a long time, you notice an elderly store owner struggling to carry boxes out to the trash. You walk over. Since you don't speak Dutch, you signal that you want to help. He understands and willingly accepts your assistance. Afterwards, he takes you inside and gives you a meal of herring, onions, freshly-baked bread, and a glass of beer.

The conversation is limited until you notice a familiar title on his bookshelf. On the spine are the Hebrew letters סִדּוּר spelling "siddur," prayer book. You know that you are in the shop of a fellow Jew, and you begin speaking *Yiddish*. Mr. Goudsmit gives you a job and a place to sleep in the back of the store. You work hard and save your money to buy a boat ticket to America.

Just when you are ready to depart, news reaches you of the conditions of the Jews of Poland under the Nazi occupation. Hearing stories of beatings and murders, you are desperately concerned about your family in Cracow. Now you must make a difficult decision: You can leave for America or stay in Holland where you may be able to help your family.

*If you decide to continue to America,
turn to page 60.*

*If you choose to stay in Holland,
turn to page 61.*

35

You feel good about your decision to join the RAF. You've got to do your part to defeat this modern *Haman,* or you will always feel like a traitor to yourself and your people. You would like to train as a pilot; however, the British won't allow this because they don't approve of Polish Jews becoming officers in their air force.

You become a gunner in a bomber and volunteer for as many missions as possible, wanting to do everything you can to stop the Nazis before they conquer all of Europe and kill every Jew.

During one especially hazardous mission, your airplane is hit by anti-aircraft fire, and the entire crew leaves the stricken aircraft by parachute. As you drift down over Nazi-occupied France, you wonder what awaits you on the ground.

If you are met by German troops and captured, turn to page 62.

If French Maquis members find you first, turn to page 63.

36

When you finally arrive in New York City, you have very little money and no friends. You turn to the *Hebrew Immigrant Aid Society* to get help finding a place to live and a job. They are able to give you some assistance, but you discover, to your dismay, that some American Jews are not pleased that you and other European Jewish refugees are arriving in the United States. They think that your accent and different ways will reflect badly on them, that non-Jewish Americans will look upon all Jews as foreigners.

HIAS is able to offer you two options for the immediate future: You can work in a small store on the Lower East Side of Manhattan where you live, or you can take a janitor's job with "Aufbau," a German-Jewish newspaper published in the city.

If you choose to work in the store,
turn to page 64.

If you decide to take the job as janitor,
turn to page 65.

37

During the time that you have lived in Berlin, the Schlechts have been your neighbors. You have visited in their apartment and have had long and friendly conversations with them. Once when you were sick, Frau Schlecht even came over to your room and nursed you back to health. You are sure that these kind, middle-aged Germans will do what they can to help you leave the country and reach neutral Sweden.

Your request is met with a completely unexpected response. "I remember 1918," Herr Schlecht tells you. "We were devastated when we lost the war; our pride was gone. And all because you accursed Jews sold us out to the French and the British. All you wanted to do was make profits from the munitions industry; you didn't care about patriotism and honor. Everything that has happened to us since then has been your fault. 'Verfluchte Juden!' Hateful Jews! I'll help you. I'll give you some help you'll never forget. Heil Hitler!"

Herr Schlecht turns you over to the *Gestapo*. You are held in a dark jail cell for a week. Then, you are pushed roughly out of your cell, down the street, and straight toward a train. There is little hope. The only question is whether you will be sent south to Dachau near Munich or east to Theresienstadt near Prague.

*If you are sent to Dachau,
turn to page 66.*

*If Theresienstadt is your destination,
turn to page 67.*

38

Disguising yourself as a peasant, you travel southward through Germany to the town of Regensburg, constantly alert to army and police patrols that are checking identity papers. Even though you have taken the documents of a dead *Aryan* German, you doubt that you could really bluff your way through a thorough check. Fortunately, you are never challenged.

Once in Regensburg, you sign up as a crew member on a barge that is headed down the Danube River, which flows past Vienna and through the middle of Budapest. Because the barge is carrying supplies to the German army in Austria, it is able to pass along the river without intensive scrutiny, and you finally set foot on the levee on the Pest side of the Danube. Since Hungary is not under German control, you feel much safer than before. In Budapest, you seek out some distant relatives and arrange to stay with them.

Turn to page 13.

39

In the early days of Nazi Germany, you had often gone boating with friends on the Havel River near Potsdam. Those sailing experiences now appear to be your only hope for escape. Traveling only at night and hiding during the day, you sneak away from Berlin and move slowly toward the Baltic Sea. Unsure of where you are going, you are frightened by every unfamiliar sound. Three times you fling yourself into ditches at the side of the road to avoid being seen. Finally, you reach the little seaside town of Barth. After scouting around, you steal a small sailboat from the beach, push it into the water, and head north.

The night is dark, and no one sees you. By daybreak, you spot an island. The flag on the schoolhouse is clearly not German; it appears to be red with a white cross on it. You take a chance and land there, and, to your great relief, you discover that you are in the Danish village of Gedser. You could not have navigated a better course if you had been an experienced sailor. The Danes help you reach Copenhagen, where you find the Great Synagogue on Krystalgade and appeal to its members for aid. They take you in and employ you at their Home for the Aged, next door to the synagogue where the old people also *daven,* morning and evening services.

Despite the German occupation, the Jews of Denmark are still safe. But, in August 1943, rumors spread that you will all be arrested. Many Danish Jews begin to think about trying to leave Denmark.

If you decide to stay with the old people,
turn to page 68.

If you leave with most of the Danish Jews,
turn to page 69.

40

The question is how to hide. Berlin is the capital of the *Third Reich,* a city full of police and soldiers. Everyday, one hears stories of Jews who have been turned over to the *Gestapo* by "friends" who had promised to conceal and protect them. You have made many good friends during the years that you have studied in the city, but now you are not sure whom you can trust.

On the other hand, no one can survive alone for long. To buy food, you must stand in long lines and produce proper identification; stolen or forged papers are spotted easily, and their users arrested. The same is true of housing; it's impossible to rent a room without risking discovery. Besides, where would you get money, now that Jews cannot obtain work?

You think about your non-Jewish friends. There were some people at the university who were more cordial than others. Perhaps you ought to trust them; what choice do you have?

Yet you are unsure of some of these people; in any case, you don't want to endanger their lives by asking them to hide you. Perhaps a Christian church will assist you. This may be a better idea.

If you ask for help from your non-Jewish university friends, turn to page 70.

If you decide to seek help from a Christian church, turn to page 71.

41

The train trip from Vilna to Moscow takes twenty-four hours. You are scared out of your wits. Here you are, racing eastward through Russia to an unknown destination with only an aged *chasidic* rabbi and his family to protect you. You confess your fear to Rabbi Kalisch, who simply puts his hand on your shoulder and says: "I know. Have faith."

During your few days in Moscow, you must buy expensive, non-kosher food—that's all you can find—and you are harassed by anti-Semitic police. Finally, however, you leave on the Trans-Siberian Railway. For eleven days, the train chugs across Russia, through Omsk to Irkutsk and finally to Vladivostok. The trip is not uncomfortable, but you are tense, still afraid that, at any point, you could be pulled off and shot or sent to a labor camp.

In Vladivostok, you must wait in a hotel until the ice in the harbor thaws. Finally, a small, rusty Japanese freighter takes you across the Sea of Japan and into the port of Kobe.

You are met there by Alex Triguboff of the Jewish community and settled in a dormitory. The floors are covered with soft tatami mats, and you eventually rest comfortably without fear. But your visa is only for temporary transit. You learn that your entire group must soon leave for the Chinese city of Shanghai. You know that, when you arrive in Shanghai, you will still have important decisions to make.

If you choose to look for a job,
turn to page 72.

If you decide to go to school,
turn to page 73.

42

The 106th Division, which you have joined, is a family camp composed of hundreds of Jewish men, women, and children. Its leader, Simon Zorin, believes that the most important thing one can do is save Jewish lives. "For us," he explains, "it's even more important than fighting the Germans. Many other people can fight. Only we can save Jews."

Russian resistance fighters in the camp disagree. They argue that supporting civilians takes needed resources away from fighting units. Zorin counters that saving lives is just as important. There are long and heated discussions between Zorin and the Russian leaders. It's a stand-off. The Russians leave; everyone realizes that they will no longer provide food and protection for the group. Fortunately, Jewish partisan units in the vicinity take their place and provide for your needs. You call these units "modern *Hasmoneans*," and occasionally you accompany them on raids into the neighboring district to collect food for the family camp.

On these raids, everyone fears the Haidamaks, anti-Semitic Ukrainians, who give the Germans information that will lead to the death of Jews. On one raid, you discover that these informers have, indeed, alerted the Germans. However, you learn this awful news too late—you have walked into an ambush. Only by fighting fiercely and courageously do you and some of your friends survive and return to camp.

But you have been wounded seriously in the left leg. With no hospital, there is nothing to do but amputate your shattered limb and hope that you recover.

Turn to page 74.

43

In the Narocz Forest, you meet armed partisan units led by Chaim Lazar and Abba Kovner. They have named one of their groups "The Vengeance" because they intend to exact a heavy price from the hated Germans. After acceptance into the group, you are given some elementary military training. Then you go on the attack. One night you ambush a German convoy. Explosives that you have planted in the road set several trucks on fire, and your machine gun bullets kill many German soldiers. You race away from the massacre, sickened by the deaths you have caused. Revenge is not sweet but brutal. You much prefer those missions that involve blowing up train tracks and bridges.

The peasants are afraid of your units and give you food, but it is difficult to secure enough weapons. The Germans cut off your supply. Anti-Semitic Russian partisans hope you meet some misfortune. Still, you will never give up. You remember the words of the famous poem, "Zog nit keynmol oz du gehst den letzen weg," Never say you walk the final road. You all conclude that you will fight on, to the death if necessary. You are uncertain, however, if you will continue your fighting in the forest or if you will leave that area.

If you decide to leave the Narocz Forest area, turn to page 75.

If you choose to continue hiding there, turn to page 76.

44

While escape seems almost impossible, you and some other inmates determine that you must try. You begin to dig a tunnel from your barracks toward the barbed wire fence and the forest beyond. It is dangerous. If you are detected, you will die a slow and agonizing death. Still you persist, slowly, quietly, hiding the dirt you remove from the tunnel in the rafters of your building.

Some inmates argue that living in the camp is, at least, predictable. They would rather not risk dying in the forest. But you and your friends are convinced that the day is coming soon when the Nazis will murder all the inmates of the camp. You are sure that the tunnel is your only path to life.

After three months of digging, you open the other end of the tunnel. It is exactly as you planned it, far enough beyond the barbed wire so that you can escape undetected. Without hesitation, your group flees out the tunnel into the woods. Later, you hear that you left just in time; all the other inmates were killed within days.

The further away you get from the camp, the safer you will be. You consider heading east toward Russia. However, a long trek like that would be very dangerous. Perhaps it would be safer to find a place of refuge nearby.

If you choose to travel eastward,
turn to page 77.

If you decide to remain nearby,
turn to page 78.

45

Knowing that you would be the cause of many innocent deaths as reprisal for escaping from Plaszow was the greatest factor in your decision to stay in the camp.

As the Russian army advances, the Germans close down the camp and move you, first to Auschwitz and finally to Bergen-Belsen. It is there that you are liberated by British troops on April 15, 1945—a date you'll never forget!

Refugee Jews flood into the camp, and rumor has it that some former Nazis, pretending to be Jews to escape punishment, are among them. You and the other Jews try to find these masqueraders and turn them over to the British. One evening, for example, you begin a discussion with someone you suspect. "I understand that we are both from Cracow. I wonder if you knew any of my friends before the war. I was particularly close to someone named *Lechah Dodi.*" The other person responds affirmatively: *"Lechah Dodi!* Sure! I knew him well." You've captured a collaborator! He is arrested and taken off to prison by British soldiers.

A while after the liberation of Bergen-Belsen, you are able to return to Cracow. You are now a free person with freedom of choice. You can plunge back into Jewish life, or you can hold off for a while and think about what to do.

If you decide to resume a Jewish life without further delay,
turn to page 79.

If you choose to take time to contemplate your future,
turn to page 80.

46

It takes a long time to arrange your escape through the sewers. You must learn the map of these underground passages. One wrong turn could be fatal. Even if you survived, you could possibly end up back in the ghetto. You spend some of your precious money to bribe a Polish policeman to guard the exit on the outside and help you once you have emerged.

On a dark night, you slip into this subterranean maze and slither through the pipes. Filth and refuse rise to your hips, and the smell is overwhelming. Only your determination to live keeps you from fainting.

When you reach the end of the tunnel, you see a ladder reaching up to street level. You stop for a moment, praying that nothing will go wrong. Then, you climb up to the street and look around. The Polish policeman is there. He saunters over to greet you; his greeting, however, is the barrel-end of his rifle. He arrests you and turns you over to the Germans. "I caught this filthy Jew crawling around in the sewers. Take him away!"

The *SS* troops take you to the camp at Treblinka, where the crematorium smokestack is topped with a Star of David and where a sign proclaims "Judenstadt," Jewish state. You realize that you have been brought to a village of death.

Turn to page 81.

47

With the medical training you had in Berlin, you are able to find work in the Jewish community. You serve as an apprentice, continuing your education under the guidance of an older physician. As the Germans reduce the size of the ghetto in Cracow, the conditions of life deteriorate: less food, more crowding, poorer sanitation, and, especially, more disease. Leaving the ghetto becomes more urgent for you every day.

When you finally decide to flee from the ghetto, you turn to the doctor who has been training you and outline an original plan for escape. The doctor understands how painful the decision is to you, torn between staying with your people and saving your life. He offers assistance in helping you get out so that you may be part of the Jewish future.

One day, just before dawn, you are given an injection which puts you into a coma. From all outward appearances, you are dead. You are placed on the cart which carries typhus victims out of the ghetto. The German sentries are afraid of catching this dread disease and step aside as the funeral cart rolls toward the cemetery. Your plan is working.

As arranged, the cart attendants take your body off the pile and hide it in a burned-out building. When the injection wears off, you wait until nightfall and then join the "Armia Ludowa," part of the Polish resistance. The resistance can hide you either in the countryside or in Warsaw.

If you decide to hide in the countryside, turn to page 82.

If you choose to go to Warsaw and take your chances in a big city, turn to page 83.

48

You leave the city on a barge which is traveling south along the Duna River. Concealed under bags of potatoes, you can hardly breathe, but, at least, you've escaped the net which Adolf Eichmann has thrown over Budapest's Jewish community. You were right in believing that the Germans would never accept the Swedish papers. After a while, they arrested many people with such documents and deported them to Auschwitz. Eichmann threatened to kill Wallenberg, eventually forcing him into hiding.

Your ship finally ties up at the Black Sea port of Odessa, where you notice something unusual. A group of Jewish children sitting on the dock, eating hard rolls and cheese, arouses your curiosity. You learn from one of the adults that these are Polish-Jewish children headed, with their adult guides, for the Iranian city of Teheran. They have been formally converted to Catholicism in order to be accepted into the camps where members of the Polish army-in-exile are living. It is understood that they will return to Judaism after the war.

If you decide to join this group to help save the children from further difficulties and persecution,
turn to page 84.

If, after learning that the Iranian border has been blocked, you choose to find another way to save the children,
turn to page 85.

49

For six months, all goes well. The masquerade of Swedish citizenship appears to be succeeding. Then, all of a sudden, Adolf Eichmann orders the *SS* troops to disregard Wallenberg's documents and to arrest anyone thought to be a Jew. Papers or no papers, you are all herded into the *Umschlagplatz* and crammed into a train headed for Auschwitz.

Just before the train leaves, a distinguished man drives up in a car bearing a red and white flag. He leaps out and rushes up to the German commander. "I am Charles Lutz," he says, "consul general from Switzerland. Some of the people you are about to deport are Swiss. Unless you let them go, there will be a major international problem." (Years later, you learn that Lutz had simply made up his list to save Jews. He is considered one of the "Chasidei Umot Haolam," one of the "Righteous People from among the Nations of the World," honored at *Yad Vashem* in Jerusalem.)

The *SS* officer and Lutz check each name. A number of people are removed from the train and taken to safe places known as "Swiss Houses." You hold your breath, hoping that you will be among them, but you are not. The door to the cattle car slams shut, the bolt clanks, and you hear the snap of the lock. You are on your way to the dread camp at Auschwitz.

If you decide to take your chances at Auschwitz, knowing that you will soon be liberated by the advancing Russian army, turn to page 86.

If you decide to escape, turn to page 87.

50

It takes several weeks to make the trip from Budapest into Russia. Fierce fighting between the retreating Russian army and the advancing Germans continues all around you. You join long lines of refugees and take advantage of the confusion to avoid patrols and escape the Germans. Finally, you pass beyond the area of intense fighting, feeling a bit more secure for the first time in many days.

You present yourself to the Russian authorities and offer to do any kind of work. They put you on a train and send you to a factory in Siberia. There, you spend the war years making rifles for the Russian army. The work is hard and the hours are long, but at least you are safe. For the moment, that is the only thing that counts.

After the war, you return to Budapest and then to Cracow. The death of Jewish life there is simply too much for you to bear. With no reason for you to stay, you make your way to a Displaced Persons camp run by the American army in southern Germany. There, a young military chaplain named Eugene Lipman helps you and other refugees start over, taking care of your immediate needs and encouraging you to plan for your future.

Among those plans, you think about returning to school. Because you are very impressed by Rabbi Lipman and his work, you consider attending a rabbinical seminary. Yet you still look back upon your early medical studies.

If you decide to become a rabbi,
turn to page 88.

If you elect to become a doctor,
turn to page 89.

51

With the help of Rudolf Kastner of the *Judenrat* and some of his non-Jewish allies, you are provided with forged documents. These papers describe you as a non-Jewish worker.

You live with a Christian Hungarian family. They do not know your true identity and think of you as another of the many people whose homes were destroyed by the fighting. Every day, you leave your rented quarters and do whatever odd jobs you can find. There are others like you, looking for employment, unable to find regular jobs, and so you blend in.

About twice each week, however, you cross over the Arpad Bridge and take a parcel of food to the wall of the Jewish ghetto in Pest. Although you are in hiding, you cannot abandon those unfortunate Jews who are trapped in the ghetto. Smuggling food to them is one way to help. You follow an irregular schedule so that no one will notice you. However, after a few months, you realize you are being followed. This can only mean that the *Arrow Cross* is suspicious. If you do not stop the smuggling, you risk arrest. You must consider your dilemma and make a quick decision.

If you decide to return to the ghetto, committing yourself to your people, turn to page 90.

If you decide to remain in Hungary and hide outside the city of Budapest, turn to page 91.

If you elect to find and join a unit of the Jewish resistance, turn to page 140.

52

You look around the cattle car for some small hint on how to escape. Suddenly, you notice that one of the corpses, an old man, is still holding a gnarled walking stick in his right hand. You grasp this stout staff and, after dark, pry loose some of the lower slats on the side of the car. While the train is not moving very quickly at this time, it will still take a great deal of luck to squeeze through the opening in the slats, drop to the ground, and avoid the scrutiny of the guards who ride with machine guns on top of each train car.

You gather your courage and make the move, hitting the ground and rolling quickly away from the tracks. A spray of machine gun fire follows you, but the shaking of the train disrupts the aim. You are free.

You slip cautiously through the countryside, wandering until you come to a farmhouse where you are given shelter in the barn and a loaf of bread and some cheese to eat. The farmer has saved your life. While you are eating, three others join the farmer, whisper for a few moments, and then come into the barn. They point rifles at you, demanding to know who you are. After you have told them your story, they lower their weapons and laugh: "You are in France. We're members of the *Maquis;* we thought you were a German spy. Come with us. We'll see that you find some friends."

Turn to page 148.

53

When the train finally arrives at its destination, you discover that you have entered the dreadful world of Birkenau near Auschwitz. Your group is marched past an *SS* officer who points some prisoners to the left and others to the right. You are young and strong and are selected to be among those who will live. The others are headed directly to the gas chambers and death.

You are assigned to work in a munitions factory for twelve hours a day. Despite the risk of instant death, you smuggle small amounts of ammunition out of the camp and into the hands of the partisans. A few workers who do this are discovered and hanged in a public ceremony, designed to discourage anyone else from this activity. However, that does not stop you.

When the Russian army advances close to Birkenau in November 1944, the camp is evacuated, and you are marched to the Ravensbrück camp near Berlin, then to Leipzig, and finally to Dachau. From Dachau you are finally liberated by the American army on April 29, 1945.

You are sent to the Displaced Persons camp at Feldafing, but soon you must decide where you will settle. You have decided to stay in southern Germany, in Munich where Hitler first began his public career. Your presence here will testify to the world that Hitler failed, that Jews and Judaism have survived despite the worst terror that the world could offer. For that testimony, you are proud and grateful.

END

54

Your new hiding place is inside a huge crate in a warehouse in the Bloemenmarket along the Herengracht. Dutch patriots and resistance members found it for you and helped you move there one dark, rainy night. There is little room in this packing box, and you must be absolutely quiet during the day, lest one of the workers becomes suspicious. Still, it is a hiding place, and you are determined to survive. And survive you do.

You are finally able to emerge into the world when Allied troops liberate the Netherlands on May 6, 1945. It is only then that you discover the full extent of the disaster that has struck European Jewry. Six million dead? You can hardly believe or comprehend. "Why," you think, "did God allow such a slaughter to take place?" For a very short time, you cannot believe that God exists or that any God that exists really cares about what happens to people.

The crisis in your faith is suddenly replaced by the determination that Hitler will never have the final victory. Jews have survived, and they will survive. You will make sure of that. With restored faith, you become a leading member of the liberal Jewish congregation in Amsterdam. With your enthusiasm, Jewish life in the Netherlands and throughout western Europe will have a future. That mission gives purpose to your life, and you are satisfied.

END

55

With the help of Dutch resistance members, you are smuggled just outside Amsterdam and hidden in a farm house on the Stadskanaal. A garret window provides a little light. Reading has always been your passion, and now you have plenty of time and good books to pass that time. You are also able to indulge your other love, sketching and drawing.

When the Allied armies liberate Holland in May 1945, you emerge from your hiding place and return to school. Soon you are able to journey to the United States to join cousins in northern Illinois. In a short time you adjust to American ways and improve your knowledge of the English language. You are accepted at the University of Wisconsin where you study architecture. It is during these years that you meet the famed American architect, Frank Lloyd Wright, and spend time learning your chosen craft at his center called Taleisin.

Finally, you establish your own architectural practice in Madison, Wisconsin, and spend your days designing buildings. You are especially happy when asked to plan private homes, recalling how awful it was to live in a little attic in Amsterdam. Some years later, you relate the story of your younger days, hoping it will convince others to build a world in which another Holocaust cannot happen.

END

56

The Germans are smarter than you thought. They know that many people, including Jews, are hiding in the Paris sewers, and they set out to catch you. It's really very simple in some cases: They flood the underground tunnels, either drowning the hiding Jews or forcing them out into the open. When Frenchmen who are collaborating with the Nazis tell the *SS* troops where to find your hiding place, you are taken prisoner.

With your hands above your head, you are marched into the center of the city and shoved rudely into the "Velodrome d'Hiver," a sports stadium used in winter for bicycle racing. If this were a winter day and you had come to watch the bicycle racing, you would have enjoyed yourself. But today there are nearly 13,000 Jews crammed into a building which was designed to hold only 2,500; it is unbearably hot; food, toilets, and medical help are unavailable. The stench of crowded bodies, sick people, and human waste is unbelievable. People react in different ways: Some scream and wail; others curl up silently in resignation; a few try to figure out an escape route—impossible. Here and there, someone lies dead. You wonder if they are the lucky ones.

After several days, you are thrown on a bus headed for the detention camp of Drancy, just a few miles north of Paris.

If your trip there occurs without incident,
turn to page 97.

If, however, your bus has an accident,
turn to page 98.

57

You crouch behind the tombstones in the cemetery in the Montmartre section of Paris. You pass the grave of Emile Zola which you consider too close to the entrance for safety. Finally you conceal yourself behind a tomb that is away from the entrance. Watching, hardly breathing, you freeze as an *SS* patrol searches the bushes outside the graveyard. But you are safe. Despite the death's-heads that adorn their uniforms, these *SS* troopers are afraid of entering a cemetery. As they march away, you sigh with relief. But your ordeal is hardly over.

You have no food, no shelter, no friends, nowhere to turn, nowhere to hide. You can sneak out at night to scavenge in garbage cans and steal food from nearby houses, but you discover a new danger. There are frequent funerals at the cemetery; you fear that you will be spotted and turned in to the German authorities.

After one particularly large funeral, you notice a nun lingering in the cemetery. She appears to be praying at other graves, but, when all the other people have left, she heads directly for you. You are nearly paralyzed with fear. There is nothing you can do but stand up: "Good afternoon, Sister."

She introduces herself as Mother Marie. "I know that you are a Jew. Come with me. We'll arrange to hide you." Her offer lifts your spirits. Previously, you were considering the possibility of fleeing on your own to Switzerland; now, you have an alternative.

*If you go with Mother Marie,
turn to page 99.*

*If you decide to flee to Switzerland,
turn to page 100.*

58

The camp at Gurs is nestled in the foothills of the Pyrenees, very close to the border with Spain. Under normal circumstances, you might have come here for a vacation—beautiful scenery, clean air and water, a lovely spot to visit. But now, it's quite a different story.

Into this internment camp, the French friends of Germany have crammed perhaps 15,000 Jews, far more than the camp can accommodate. As a result, people sleep out in the open, on the muddy ground. If it rains, you get soaked; if it snows, you may even freeze to death. There is hardly enough food to keep you alive. There are no toilets except those which the inmates improvise; no medical help is available. Within months of your arrest, 2,000 of the inmates have died as a result of the unbearable conditions.

You survive, you are certain, only because you have come here with a large group of friends, friends you trust, friends who will protect and help each other. So, it becomes a dilemma when a sympathetic camp guard suggests that it would be to your advantage to leave your friends and look out for yourself.

If you stay with your friends,
turn to page 101.

If you take the advice of the guard and
separate yourself from the others,
turn to page 102.

59

Even though the Vichy French are less vigilant than the Germans who control the Occupied Zone, traveling without any official papers is almost impossible. You've got to find a way.

While you try to figure out how to get to Marseilles, a German courier on a motorcycle appears. About fifty yards from where you are hiding, his vehicle hits a rut in the road and flips over. The rider's helmet flies off; he lands on his head and lies immobile in the road. You look around; no one else is there. You dash over to him, but you cannot tell whether he is dead or unconscious. His misfortune benefits you. You strip off his uniform and put it on. You are now a German courier while he now wears the clothing of a fugitive.

With his motorcycle and his official papers, the trip to Marseilles is easy. You pass through beautiful countryside and eat lunch under the famous bridge at Avignon. Once in Marseilles, you discard the motorcycle and the uniform, knowing you would never find the resistance and a way out of France dressed like a German.

If you choose to search for the resistance for help,
turn to page 103.

If you decide to hide in the dock area of Marseilles,
turn to page 104.

60

With some money you've saved working for Mr. Goudsmit, you get to New York. When you arrive in the city, a representative from *HIAS* meets you and gives you a letter from a cousin in St. Louis. Your cousin owns a men's clothing store and is willing to have you work there and live with his family. The *HIAS* agent gives you some American money and puts you on the train. As you look out the train window, you think to yourself: "This is a beautiful country, and so large. In Europe we would have crossed four countries, but here we are still in America!"

Your cousin and his family meet you at the station in St. Louis. At first they seem very nice, but then you overhear the children laughing at your strange ways. "No 'rachmonis' here, no mercy," you say in a whisper. That proves to be true. At the store, you work like a slave, dragging merchandise up and down, sweeping the floor, washing, scrubbing, doing every chore. When two weeks have passed, you ask your cousin about a salary. "What? You want money, too? Isn't it enough that my wife and I give you shelter and food? Would you rather be back in Poland?"

Through the grapevine, you hear that a German-Jewish refugee has the same kind of business in a little town in Illinois, just across the Mississippi River from St. Louis. He needs a helper and is willing to pay. You decide to take the job with him.

Turn to page 105.

61

You try to get information about your family in Cracow, but no one you have been able to contact in Holland seems to know what is going on in Poland. You pay so much attention to the news from Eastern Europe that you are unaware of the massing of German armies near the Dutch border. Suddenly, on May 10, 1940, the Germans invade Holland, and four days later the country surrenders. Now you find yourself trapped in occupied territory.

At first, the Nazi occupation doesn't seem too bad. There are anti-Jewish laws, but your life is not in danger. You even find a job as an apprentice in a diamond cutting shop.

In February 1941, Jews in south Amsterdam attack a German police patrol. In retaliation, the Nazis start to round up Jews and deport them to concentration camps. For eighteen months, you are safe. Then, when a Dutch collaborator denounces you, you are arrested by the *Gestapo* and taken to Westerbork, a transit camp where people are held for only a short time before being sent to camps farther east. Most Jews from Westerbork are sent directly to Auschwitz.

However, you learn that it is possible to volunteer to go to Bergen-Belsen with a group of Dutch Jews who have been recruited to teach diamond cutting to the Nazis. With the knowledge you have acquired in the diamond cutting shop and your natural talent, you consider this alternative.

If you risk deportation to Auschwitz,
turn to page 107.

If you volunteer to teach at Bergen-Belsen,
turn to page 108.

62

As you hit the ground, you realize that the navigator of the airplane has landed near you. You crawl over to him but discover he has been killed by a bullet in the chest. You take his identification tags so that the German soldiers will not know that you are a Jew.

When you are taken prisoner, the Germans believe that you are a British officer and send you to a special prisoner-of-war camp. They never suspect your Polish-Jewish origin, and you manage to survive the rest of the war. When you are finally liberated in 1945, you return to England only to learn that your entire family has been killed in Auschwitz. You are totally alone in the world.

You spend several months trying to figure out what to do. No place feels like home. The British are good to you, but they're not family. You are at loose ends; you seem to have no roots anywhere.

Finally, you join the British Overseas Airways Corporation as a flight officer and spend the rest of your days working on passenger planes going around the world. You end your days feeling like a person without a country, never belonging anywhere—a permanent refugee.

END

63

You ou are smuggled by the *Maquis* across the English Channel and report back to your unit. Your commanding officer thinks you have taken enough risks, but you persist: "Sir, I must fight; Hitler is my personal enemy." You continue to fly dangerous missions. For your bravery, you are eventually awarded the Distinguished Flying Cross.

With the war over, you must decide what to do with your future. You receive a call from Irwin Schindler at Service Airways in the United States, telling you he is recruiting Jewish aircrews. Although he will not tell you the details over the trans-Atlantic telephone, something about the offer intrigues you. You go to the training base in California. Here you discover that you and other war veterans are training to become the core of an air force which will go to the new State of Israel. You are very excited; fighting for a Jewish state is exactly what you want to do.

Schindler sends you and several others with a Palestinian named Elie Schalit to Czechoslovakia, where you pick up some used planes. They have been purchased by the *Haganah* and are filled with crates marked "Agricultural Implements" and "Used Machinery." Schalit winks at you and shows you that the "implements and machinery" are really guns and ammunition to defend the new Jewish nation. You fly the planes and their cargo to an airport near Tel Aviv and participate in the War of Independence. You are so happy in the Israel Air Force that you continue as a career officer. You've finally found the place where you belong.

END

64

You take the job as a store clerk on Manhattan's Lower East Side and spend four years living and working among the Russian Jews who live in this area. At least these Jews understand your problems. After all, they and their parents had to flee tsarist pogroms and persecutions in Eastern Europe a generation earlier. When you talk about your anger, your fears for the safety of the family you have left behind, and your uncertainty in this new land, they understand.

Yet, the more you learn about what is happening in Europe as German armies sweep through the old *Pale of Settlement,* the more you conclude that this situation is different. No one has ever before tried to kill every Jew in the world. Something totally unique is happening, and only those who have experienced it personally can really understand. Finally, you feel you must be among refugees from the Nazis. You move to Washington Heights, a section along the Hudson River where many German-Jewish refugees have settled. On *Shabbat* morning, you find the services, even the way the Hebrew is pronounced, very familiar. After the services you meet people who have had many of the same experiences as you. This is where you will spend the rest of your life. This is your new home.

END

65

Your job as janitor with the German-Jewish newspaper "Aufbau" is hardly what you expected when you attended medical school in Berlin. Yet, "Aufbau" is the most outspoken publication protesting the events in Europe; the editorials and articles continually urge the American government to take a more active role in preventing the massacre of Jews in the concentration camps.

When you arrive at work one morning, the office is buzzing with discussion and argument. A big demonstration against the Nazis is planned for Madison Square Garden.

Some think a public protest rally is the wrong way to help the European Jews. Rather, they argue, a private, diplomatic strategy will be more effective in persuading the American State Department to save as many Jews as possible. Through the *American Jewish Committee,* these people try to influence President Roosevelt and his advisors.

But, even from brief press releases that come to "Aufbau" and the many rumors in the Jewish community, you decide that this is the wrong tactic. From what you can learn about *Breckinridge Long* and the State Department's attitude in general, you realize that quiet pressure and private efforts won't get the American government to help the Jews.

Membership in the *American Jewish Congress* suits you better. You feel good as you march down Fifth Avenue carrying a sign protesting the massacre of European Jewry, stirred by the speeches of *Rabbi Stephen S. Wise.* You decide: "These public protests may not save the Jews of Europe, but, at least, I shall have done what I could. Let the world know that Jews will fight for their rights and their lives."

END

66

When you leave the train at Dachau, it is late at night, but the station platform is as bright as day; huge lights glare at you from the top of tall poles. *SS* troopers beat you mercilessly to hurry you along; other soldiers hold snarling dogs straining at the end of leather leashes. You stumble along the platform and go down several steps into a long, shuffling line.

Most people look down, depressed and dejected. They are terrified, and you are, too. In fact, you have never been as frightened in your life. But, you decide that the one thing the Nazis cannot steal from you is your pride, and you stand erect and walk with confidence.

Before you, an officer holding a riding crop scans each of you in turn. A little flick to the left puts people in one group; a slight motion to the right directs others to that side. There seems to be no reason for his choices; everything depends, it appears, solely on his mood and whim at that particular second.

The group to which you are assigned is marched off to a processing section of the concentration camp. Tomorrow morning you will be assigned work to do in the camp. Exhausted, you fall asleep on the hard, wooden rack that is your bed.

If you are assigned work like other prisoners, turn to page 111.

If you are singled out for the Sonderkommando, turn to page 112.

67

Theresienstadt is considered the showplace of German concentration camps. Compared to most, this is probably true. However, it is still a prison; still a place where Jews and others suffer greatly; still a place of torture, disease, terror, and death. When you enter the camp, you feel hopeless. Only one fate awaits you—a horrible, senseless death.

A few days later, after the long day of hard labor, you are invited into a neighboring barracks. You are so tired that you almost decline the invitation, but the other inmates are insistent, and so you go. There, you find a small, gray-bearded, bald man sitting in the center of a circle of prisoners. He is talking intensely in the kind of German you used to hear from your professors at the university. You listen intently and discover that he is teaching Greek philosophy.

After the lecture, you inquire: "Who is this person?" "That's Rabbi Dr. Leo Baeck. Before the war, he was the chief Liberal rabbi of Berlin. During World War One, he was a chaplain in the German army. He could have left Germany in 1938 or 1939, but he stayed with his congregation and insisted on coming here with us. Everyday, he teaches a class after work. Coming here keeps us all alive and alert."

After that experience, you sit quietly in a corner, thinking to yourself: "If Rabbi Baeck can have enough hope to teach philosophy, I can have enough hope to survive."

Later, you are transferred to another camp.

*If you are sent to Ravensbrück,
turn to page 113.*

*If you end up in Dachau,
turn to page 114.*

68

Grateful for the shelter and protection the Jewish community of Copenhagen had given you, you felt obligated to do something for them in return. Your *mitzvah* has been to work as a volunteer in the Home for the Aged, taking care of the elderly Jews. You have come to love many of them. They have become your adopted family. Now that the Nazis are threatening to deport all of Denmark's Jews, you cannot leave these dear, older people to the terrors that you observed during "Kristallnacht." You determine to stay with them at all costs.

Most of Denmark's Jews escape when their fellow Danes arrange to ferry them to neutral Sweden. Those among the residents of the "Jewish Old Folks Home" who can manage the trip also go, but there are some who are too frail. You choose to stay with them.

The Germans take you all to the Theresienstadt Concentration Camp. But the Danish government does not forget its Jewish citizens and finally secures permission to visit you in the camp. A number of the older people die of natural causes, but no one is sent to Auschwitz.

Your own hope for survival is cut short, however, when, one day, you begin to cough up blood. You have tuberculosis, and there is nothing that can be done for you. Gradually, you lose weight and become weaker. With your final breath, you whisper *Shema Yisrael* and close your eyes for the last time.

END

69

A German official in Denmark, George Ferdinand Dukwitz, has warned the Jewish community that the Nazis are planning to arrest all of you on Rosh Hashanah when you will all be together at synagogue services.

The Danish resistance acts quickly. The ships on which you are to be deported are blown up in the harbor, and arrangements are made to ferry nearly all of Denmark's 7,200 Jews to Sweden. You feel terrible about leaving the elderly in the "Jewish Old Folks Home," but other young people convince you that you owe more to the Jewish future, that you must survive with them. In the end, you simply have no choice; they drag you along and push you on the boat.

An entire fleet of small boats takes you and the other Danish Jews across the Öresund and into the harbor at Malmö. There, representatives of the *(American Jewish) Joint Distribution Committee* have arranged housing and food. Throughout the war, you live in southern Sweden, protected by that country's neutrality and supported by the *JDC*.

After the war, you must decide what to do with your life.

If you choose to return to Denmark and build a life for yourself there, turn to page 115.

If you decide to go as far as possible from Europe and all its terrible memories, turn to page 116.

70

By yourself, you will not survive. Therefore, you appeal to some Christian friends of yours who hide you in their attic. You can only go out of the room at night, and then only into the second floor of the house. As the months of your confinement pass, everyone in the family becomes tense. The pressure is unbearable, and you know you are responsible. If you are discovered, you and the entire family will be shot. It's happened before, just down the street, in fact. An entire German family was massacred by the *Gestapo* when a Jewish woman was found in their house.

You cannot ask your friends to accept such a burden. Before you leave their home, you tell them how much you appreciate their help, but that you cannot stay. As you walk out into the street, you hear a loud, roaring noise. You look up and see airplanes, bombers, just about to unleash an attack on Berlin. People race for bomb shelters. This is your chance. You remain on the street, hiding in the corner of a building, watching, waiting. When the bombs fall nearby, you dash out. A corpse lies in the street. You run over, grab the person's wallet, and dash back to your hiding place. The money will help, but the identity cards are more important.

You must now decide how you will try to survive the rest of the war. Like some, you can live in the ruins of the city, scavenging for food, or you can pretend to be a regular citizen, live in an apartment, and get a job.

If you decide to live in the city ruins, turn to page 117.

If you pretend to lead a normal life, turn to page 118.

71

Hitler has already eliminated many of the Christian ministers who had spoken out against the Nazi regime, but you are sure that there must be others who can help you. Their acts of defiance may be less obvious, but these are still acts of deep Christian faith and conscience.

You begin to attend services in various Lutheran and Reformed churches, hoping to find a place of refuge. When one older minister's sermon suggests he might be approachable, you decide to take the risk. After services, when the congregation has left, you speak to him in private. He tells you he will help because he remembers *Pastor Martin Niemoller* and what his colleague said about not waiting too long to protest. "If I am going to be honest to my biblical faith," the minister says, "I cannot stand idly by while my neighbor bleeds."

The minister provides you with temporary refuge in the basement of the church while he secures forged identity cards for you. Then, he offers you two options: There is a job open as caretaker in a cemetery. You could probably work there unmolested for the rest of the war. On the other hand, the Siemens Munitions Factory always needs workers. You could lose yourself among the many people employed there and survive as just another laborer.

If you decide to take the job as cemetery caretaker,
turn to page 119.

If you choose to work at the munitions factory,
turn to page 120.

72

When you present yourself to the Committee for the Assistance of European Jews in Shanghai (CFA), the employment officer asks about your previous training. You tell him that you had several years of medical school in Berlin, and he seems excited. "We can use you right here," he exclaims, "teaching other refugees about sanitary housing and proper nutrition."

You are pleased to work for the CFA because it appears to be doing very important work. Nearly 17,000 refugee Jews have crowded into a small area of Shanghai, where it is very difficult for them to find places to stay, proper food to eat, and, especially, work to do. There simply aren't many jobs. The rich *Sephardim* who head the CFA, Victor Sassoon and Silas Hardoon, spend a good deal of their own money to provide resettlement help, but even that's not enough. A little money trickles in from the *Joint Distribution Committee,* but this aid is cut off when Japan attacks Pearl Harbor.

Many of the refugees resent that no one asks their advice in running the CFA; they have no control over matters that mean a great deal to them. After a while, it appears that you cannot continue at the CFA.

*If you decide to work for a new organization
run by the refugees themselves,
turn to page 121.*

*If you choose to look for a different job,
having had enough of refugee resettlement,
turn to page 122.*

73

An entire *yeshivah* of 300 students and teachers from Mir, Poland, has also relocated in Shanghai. You decide to join their ranks. Their purpose and dedication attract you.

Every day, you leave the Hongkew district, the center of the Shanghai Jewish community, and go to the Beth Abraham Synagogue, which has been turned into a "Bet Hamidrash," a study hall. There, you and the others probe the secrets of the *Gemara* and medieval Jewish legal texts. You find the intellectual challenge exciting.

As you return from the synagogue one evening, you spot a tall, erect man wearing a German army uniform. A few well-placed questions uncover the fact that this is Colonel Joseph Meisinger, the notorious "Butcher of Worms (Germany)," who has come to Shanghai to convince the Japanese who control the city that they should extend Hitler's *"Final Solution"* to include the 17,000 Jewish refugees there.

When you tell Rabbi Kalisch, he and other community leaders meet with the Japanese governor. Rabbi Kalisch reminds the governor of Hitler's racial policy. "If Hitler says that only *Aryan* people have a place as leaders of the world in the future, what does that mean for you, for all Orientals?" The governor understands Rabbi Kalisch's reasoning, and Colonel Meisinger's mission is stopped.

After the war, some members of the *yeshivah* leave for Jerusalem. Others go to America, to Brooklyn, New York.

If you accompany those going to Jerusalem,
turn to page 123.

If you go with the others to America,
turn to page 124.

74

A few weeks after the Russian army recaptures Lithuania, you are summoned to appear at headquarters. As you hobble into the camp on crutches, a high-ranking officer greets you warmly and leads you to the tent of the commanding general. You are totally surprised when the general pins the Order of Lenin on your tunic, kisses you on both cheeks, and salutes. "For heroes of the Revolution like you," he explains, "nothing is too good. Now, I order you to return to Vilna. We have arranged that you will work for the Ministry of Education."

You are expected to teach about Russian government to groups of families that meet every evening in order to become better Communists. Soon, however, you realize that what you are doing is not education but propaganda—much of what you teach is not even true!

Even more troublesome is the disappearance of many well-known Jewish scholars, writers, musicians, and actors. When you try to discover where they have gone, the authorities simply don't respond. You begin to fear the worst; it's almost as if Joseph Stalin was repeating Hitler's elimination of the Jews.

These and other disturbing facts convince you that you must leave Russia.

If you decide to attempt the difficult task of obtaining an official exit permit, turn to page 125.

If you choose to simply start walking out of the country, turn to page 126.

75

Near Kobilnik, German troops try to surround your unit. More experienced partisans, however, lead your escape to an island surrounded by muddy swamps through which you must wade, often in water up to your hips. You cut off branches and crawl across them so that you do not sink into the deepest water. Exhausted, you finally pull yourself onto the dry land of the island.

With a burst of humor, you call this island "America." It is wildly overgrown with high grass and tall trees. On three sides you are surrounded by the swamp. On the fourth is the lake of Narocz. The Germans will not be able to penetrate your hideout.

The holiday of Chanukah falls during your stay on the island. To celebrate the festival, you collect nine containers —anything that will hold oil—and kindle the traditional lights. It makes you feel good to observe this ancient festival of freedom, and you are sure that your own liberation is on the way.

After the war, you decide that you want to be among Jewish people. Since most of the Jews of Eastern Europe were killed by the Nazis, you head for the city of Stettin where you learn that the former concentration camp of Bergen-Belsen is now an exclusively-Jewish "city." You decide to go there.

Turn to page 168.

76

In immense underground bunkers, you store food and weapons. Hundreds of partisans are able to hide in these bunkers. Air to breathe is piped in through tubes that rise above the ground in thickets and hollow tree stumps. Once, when Germans were closing in on you, you concealed the entrance of the bunker with the carcasses of dead horses, and the Germans avoided that area. Meanwhile, you are able to continue raiding German communication and transportation facilities, impeding their war effort.

In 1944, when the Russian army liberates the area, you decide to return to Poland, to your home city of Cracow. You begin the long trip, only to discover groups of bandits led by Stefan Bandera. These anti-Semitic Ukrainians will attack anyone for their own advantage, but they particularly gain satisfaction harassing Jews. You must be extraordinarily careful, traveling only at night and hiding from Bandera during the day. You are very angry that, although the war is over, your life is still in danger. The government is doing nothing to protect you. You feel you deserve more help, considering the price you have paid during the last three years.

Turn to page 166.

77

From Plaszow, you make your way first to Lvov and then to Kiev behind the Russian lines. You and your friends present yourselves to the authorities and tell them what you have done. They put you in a barracks and give you decent food, the first you have had in years. The thick potato soup and the heavy black bread are almost too rich for you to digest. However, gradually you return to health.

You tell the Russian commander that you must fight the Nazis, burning to avenge your dead family. It would seem a small sacrifice to you if you were to die in battle, as long as you were able to have the satisfaction of killing Germans first.

As a Russian soldier, you advance westward across the Ukraine and into Poland. You participate in many battles and are awarded the Defense of the Fatherland medal for your bravery. You wear this decoration very proudly on your tunic; it is a symbol of the love you feel for your family.

After the war, you settle in the city of Minsk where a Jewish orphanage has opened. You work with the children, helping them make new lives without their parents. This important work makes you feel good, and you continue to work with children for the rest of your career.

END

78

You know enough to distrust the peasants of southern Poland, who have a well-deserved reputation for anti-Semitism. Seeking refuge among them might be the same as turning yourself over to the Germans. Yet, you desperately need a place to hide.

One day, as you are passing a Catholic convent, your attention is drawn to one of the nuns. There is something strange about her. Her shoulders are too broad, her gait rather masculine, her body very muscular. You approach her, speak to her, and, indeed, realize that "she" is a man. When you tell him your story, he immediately escorts you inside the convent gate. There, you learn that he is called Oswald and that he was formerly a Jewish spy inside the Polish Nazi party. He was able to send out messages to help Jews, especially those from Mir, escape the *"Final Solution."* Eventually, his spying was discovered, and he went into hiding, disguised as a nun, here in the convent.

The nuns at the convent agree to conceal you as well. They give you false baptismal papers, identifying you as a person who has always lived in the vicinity. After changing your appearance slightly, especially by growing your hair longer, you spend the next two years at the convent, helping in the kitchen and garden, never venturing beyond the convent walls.

After the liberation, you arrange for a thanksgiving mass, praising God for the courageous nuns. "You saved my life—not once, but many times. I shall never forget. But now I must go to join my own people in Palestine."

Turn to page 129.

79

You cross the Neisse River at Görlitz and reenter Poland. From there, you ride on farmers' carts or walk until you finally reach your hometown of Cracow. Practically no Jews remain alive in Poland, but those who do somehow manage to find each other. A group has gathered in Cracow and has formed Kibbutz Gordonia, dedicated to working with the few children who are still alive.

Many of these children had been hidden by Polish Catholic families who loved and protected them, but who also hoped that they would convert to Catholicism.

You work diligently to locate these children and bring them back into Judaism. "With as many children as we have lost to the Nazi horror," you exclaim, "we cannot afford to give up even one more child."

When the children first come to live with you, they are afraid to take off the crucifixes that hang around their necks. These crosses have protected them throughout the war, and they surrender this symbol of safety very reluctantly. You and the other kibbutzniks work with them gently and patiently, recognizing that they have already had so much trouble in their young lives. A little time is all they need—and you succeed.

Months later, it is time to lead a group of them to the west. You volunteer and take them back along the same route you took on your return to Poland. You enter the gates of Bergen-Belsen—this time as a free person, leading a group of Jewish children. There is a tumultuous, hero's welcome awaiting you.

Turn to page 168.

80

Back in Cracow, you take some time for serious thinking. You feel that Judaism has nearly destroyed your life. After all, it was because you were a Jew that you could not get into a Polish university, that you lost your chance to become a doctor in Berlin, that your family was murdered, that you suffered intolerable hardships during the war, barely escaping with your life. No, Judaism has cost you dearly. Yet you do not believe that Christianity would solve your problems.

Your only option is to join the Communist party. You want to fight for the ideals of international peace and brotherhood. "Karl Marx was right," you conclude. " 'Religion is the opiate of the masses.' I've grown beyond that stage. I shall be part of the revolution of the people to bring a glorious new world into being."

When the Communists come into power in Poland, you take a job in the government Ministry of Health. You enjoy your work, but you notice that the same hatreds and jealousies still exist. Apparently, changing political systems did not eliminate prejudice.

You have failed to realize your ideals, but you remain in your job. You have committed yourself too firmly to back down now. You have cast your lot with the Communist party, and you must accept the consequences of your decision.

END

81

In Treblinka, you see a death camp in all its horror. Thousands of Jews are massacred and then burned each day. When the process slows down because there are too many Jews for the Germans to kill, some are buried alive. You cannot believe that people would act so inhumanly; even wild animals do not treat each other this way.

You notice that the *Chasidim* seem to go to their death with inner peace. Believing that this is part of God's plan or a punishment for their sins, they die, so they say, for *Kiddush Hashem.* You wonder if God wants this sacrifice. Would it not be more pleasing in heaven if you were to live to praise the Lord! The more you think, the more you conclude that you must live. You will live; you will escape; you will tell the world of the horrors of Treblinka.

On *Shabbat,* the Nazis relax their guard. Jews are occupied with their prayers and would not escape on the holy Sabbath day. You take advantage of this lapse and, together with Josef Cyrankiewicz, you wiggle through a trench under the barbed wire fence. By the time the guards miss you the next morning, you are far away from the camp.

You know that, if you can get to Switzerland, you can tell your story to people who will listen. However, such a trip will be long and dangerous since it is through German-occupied territory. It might even be impossible. Perhaps, it would be better to stay in Poland and join a partisan unit.

If you choose to attempt the trip to Switzerland,
turn to page 130.

If you decide to join the partisans,
turn to page 131.

82

In cellars, in barns, in holes dug in the ground under haystacks, in any place you can find, you hide. The farmers don't like a Jew hiding on their property because, if you are discovered, they will also be killed. But even greater than their fear is their hatred of the invading Germans. So they offer some cooperation, and you are able to keep one jump ahead of the Nazis and their anti-Semitic Polish collaborators. In this way, you survive the war.

After the war, you return to Cracow, hoping to find your family, but you learn that they have all died at Auschwitz. You do not find many Jews. There are only a few left.

While you are trying to reestablish your life in Cracow, a pogrom breaks out in the small city of Kielce. Over forty Jews are killed and many others beaten. A nine-year-old boy had told the story that he was kidnapped by Jews and taken to a cellar where he saw fifteen Christian children murdered. This lie set off the violence. Only one Polish priest, Father Henryk Werynski, speaks out from the pulpit against the pogrom, and he is quickly removed from his post. You are reminded that the Catholic Church in Poland is infected with hatred for Jews.

This realization forces you to the conclusion that you must get out of Poland. There is no future for Jews here. With the help of *Brichah,* you travel west until you reach Feldafing, a Displaced Persons camp in southern Germany. When you finally receive a visa to settle in America, you are assigned to live in Mobile, Alabama. You know nothing about this city, but, if this is the way for you to leave behind a Europe where millions of Jews have died, you'll go gladly.

Turn to page 133.

83

In Warsaw, your medical training helps you get a job at the orphanage run by Dr. Janus Korczak. Together with his band of dedicated nurses, Dr. Korczak cares for a large number of parentless children. You are glad to help.

An *SS* officer enters one day, announcing that the orphanage must move. "We are taking you in trucks to a new school, far out in the country. Be prepared to move tomorrow morning. Each person may take only one small bundle."

Korczak realizes that this is a relocation, not to a new school, but to death—the same death faced by most of the Warsaw Ghetto residents. He knows that he and the nurses could escape the transport, and, in fact, he orders you and the nurses to leave him. The nurses agree, but you cannot. "Dr. Korczak," you respond, "you took me in when I was a fugitive. I will not abandon you and, especially, I will not abandon these children, no matter what happens."

The next morning, the children, you, and Dr. Korczak are marched out and loaded into waiting trucks. The doors shut, and the vehicles start to move. A sickening smell begins to appear in the sealed compartment where you are riding. You realize that the Germans are pumping carbon monoxide gas into the truck. It will soon be over; as you lean against the wall of the truck, you smile, recalling the happy events of your life before the great tragedy befell Europe's Jews.

E N D

84

Some members of the real Polish army and their priest are also traveling with you. Unaware that you are Jewish, they do not disguise their true feelings about Jews. The priest confides to you that he will never allow the children to return to Judaism after the war, even if it means killing the adult guides. His words and the laughing agreement of the Polish soldiers teach you that these people harbor deep feelings of anti-Semitism; you can never feel safe in their presence.

As soon as possible, you repeat their hate-filled words and threats of violence to the leaders of the children's group. They are not surprised for they have heard these sentiments all along the trip. Nonetheless, they agree that you must work with them to help rescue the children and to bring them back to a Jewish life.

When you enter Teheran, you look around, scouting for some plan, some place to take the young people. As you walk through one district of the city, you notice that the stores have steps behind the sales counters; the clerks stand in sunken pits. You are curious and ask about these strange depressions.

Turn to page 134.

85

With the border closed, there is only one thing for you to do. You separate the group of Jewish children from the Polish army-in-exile members and head east. Your first priority is to get the children away from the fighting. You cross southern Russia and, with the help of local guides, make your way through the mountains of Pamir and northern Pakistan.

Before leaving Russia, however, you plant a tree. The other members of your group are astounded, wondering what you are doing. You tell them that *Choni Hame'aggel* planted a tree so that his grandchildren could have fruit, in the same way that the biblical prophet Jeremiah bought a field in Anatoth for his descendants. You want to make provisions for the future as members of the Jewish community have always done. Eventually, you reach the valley of the Indus River, a route you can follow southward to the city of Karachi on the Arabian Sea.

From Karachi, you arrange passage by ship to the Egyptian port of Suez at the southern end of the Suez Canal. When you disembark under the broiling Sinai sun, you are surprised to find trucks from the *Jewish Brigade*. The drivers tell you that a message had been sent ahead about your arrival and that they had been dispatched to take you and the children to the camp at Athlit.

Once the children are settled in the camp, you must decide what you are going to do.

If you decide to study in a yeshivah in Jerusalem,
turn to page 135.

If you choose to work on a kibbutz,
turn to page 136.

86

The rumor that the Russian army will soon liberate the camp gives you strength to carry on. Because of your previous training, you are assigned to work in the camp hospital. Conditions for you are somewhat better, but you cannot say the same for the unfortunate sick people who are brought there. The hospital is a place of death, which most inmates avoid, even when they are very ill. The doctors operate without anesthetics and perform horrible experiments on prisoners to prove the Nazi theories of Jewish racial inferiority. Even though you are forced to participate in this medical abuse of human beings, you try to remember every incident. Some day, you will tell the world about the terrible things you have seen.

One day at dawn, you awaken to a great commotion. In the distance, you hear the thudding sound of artillery. Everyone is rushed outside, counted, and then forced to march out of the camp. Anyone who dares to ask "Where are we headed?" is clubbed to death and left by the road. You bow your head and pray for strength to endure this new torture.

Turn to page 137.

87

So many people are shoved into the cattle car that you cannot even count them. There is no room to sit or lie down; you are crushed against each other with hardly enough room to breathe. The train lurches forward. For days you are trapped inside.

The cramped conditions and long journey are too much for some of the passengers, especially the older ones; many of them die. Inhumanity like this is simply unbearable. Conditions like these make you decide to escape.

An older man next to you takes his last breath and sags against the side of the car. You stare in terror at his gaping mouth and glazed eyes. You lower your eyes, looking away from his frozen face. In his hand is a walking stick, which stirs your imagination. You take his walking stick and, using it as a tool, begin to pry up the floor boards of the cattle car, little by little, splinter by splinter, until there is a hole large enough for your body. You wait until dark and lower yourself to the tracks. Fortunately, the train is moving slowly, and you are not injured as you fall to the trackbed. You huddle close to the ground; the train passes over you.

You begin walking east. If only you can make your way into the Ukraine, you can probably find a partisan unit to protect you.

After two weeks of sleeping under bushes and stealing food, you stumble upon a partisan camp. After identifying yourself to the partisans, you tell them your story. They believe what you say and accept you. They offer you the opportunity to join one of two Jewish units, the 106th Division or a unit called "The Vengeance."

If you decide to join the 106th Division, turn to page 42.

If you choose to join "The Vengeance," turn to page 43.

88

On *Tishah Be'av,* you sit on the floor of the synagogue in the DP camp and read from the Book of Lamentations in the Bible. You identify strongly with what the author of those biblical verses wrote; your life has been filled with the same agony and sadness. Because you were born and raised as a Jew, you have been persecuted and nearly killed. Because they were Jews, six million of your brothers and sisters have died. Perhaps it is time to stop being a member of this people of misery.

Then, another thought comes to you. As an infant, your parents held a ceremony welcoming you into the ancient covenant with God, a covenant that stretches back to Mount Sinai. As a Jew, you accepted the duty of living up to that covenant, of making this world better and more godly. Your job is certainly not finished; the last few years have surely proved that. You cannot step away from this obligation merely because it has been difficult and painful. You are a Jew; you must remain one.

Rabbi Lipman's influence has helped you decide to attend a rabbinical seminary in the United States. You choose to attend the Jewish Theological Seminary of America in New York and are ordained as a Conservative rabbi. You take a pulpit and spend the rest of your life teaching other people about the importance of being Jewish. It is this mission that gives your life meaning.

END

89

Even though you are very impressed with the dedication of the military chaplains, you cannot abandon your early dream of becoming a doctor. Thus you decide to complete your medical education. But where? You cannot return to Berlin; the memories are just too painful for you to live in the capital of the *Third Reich*. On the other hand, you are still not welcome in universities in Poland.

While you are trying to make a decision, stories reach you about the kindness of the Scandinavian people during the war, about how they tried to save Jews, even at great risk to themselves. You decide that you would like to live among people like that, and you enroll at the University of Oslo in Norway.

What you had heard turns out to be true. You feel comfortable among these people, and you complete your studies with high honors. You then continue your training at the Rothschild Hospital in Vienna, becoming a psychiatrist. This hospital is exclusively for Jews fleeing Eastern Europe, people whose lives you understand because you experienced many of the same terrors that still haunt them. You are able to help many of them rid themselves of guilt and anger, fear and trembling.

When your training in Vienna is finished, you return to Oslo and become a doctor at the university's psychiatric clinic. Your reputation for treating Holocaust survivors spreads across Europe, and patients come to you from many countries. Helping your fellow Jews escape their mental suffering gives you tremendous pleasure; it is as though all your own anguish prepared you for the purpose of caring for your own people. Your work is always gratifying; it is a *mitzvah*.

END

90

Returning to the ghetto places you in great danger, but these are your people, your family. You care for them, and you are proud to be among them; you are proud to be a Jew. If the world wants to kill you, at least you will die honestly and openly as a Jew, with the *Shema* on your lips. You would prefer not to be a martyr, but, should it come to that. . . .

The Germans begin to reduce the number of Jews in the ghetto. Roundups and deportations continue through the winter of 1943 and into the spring of 1944, when most of the Jews of Budapest are sent to concentration camps. Among the last to leave, you are puzzled by the delay in your deportation. But, then again, much of what has happened doesn't make any sense!

You are sent to the camp at Buchenwald where you see the sign over the gate: "Arbeit Macht Frei," Work Leads to Freedom. You've heard about this freedom through work; it really means the Germans will work you so hard that the only freedom you will find is freedom from life.

Many of the inmates slave at making shoes from, of all things, corn husks. Others have different jobs, all with long hours, little food, and very hard conditions. You are more fortunate. A fellow inmate, a friend from Budapest, offers you the opportunity to join a choir he organized at the camp.

Moreover, the Germans, upon reviewing your records, learn of your medical training and give you the chance to work in the camp hospital.

If you decide to join the choir,
turn to page 138.

If you choose to work in the hospital,
turn to page 139.

91

Southeast of Budapest lies the important agricultural center of Szeged. It is in this direction that you flee. A Hungarian friend of yours has given you the name of his cousin who owns a farm east of Szeged, near the little town of Mako. He thinks his cousin will hide you.

When you arrive at the farm, you discover that your friend was right. His cousin has been having trouble getting workers for his paprika and onion crops. He is desperate for anyone who will do the hard work of tending the onion plants and picking the paprika, a spice that seems to be the staple of any truly Hungarian diet: veal "paprikash," chicken "paprikash," everything is "paprikash."

You are grateful to the farmer-cousin for his hospitality and for the risk he takes in hiding you. You work very hard to repay his kindness. Despite your fear that the Germans will discover you, you continue to work in the fields, even making friends with many of the local citizens.

When the Russian army finally liberates this region, you expect to feel safe again. However, you soon learn that the Russian secret police are everywhere, arresting anyone whose loyalty to the new occupation army is in doubt. You are no more sure of your safety under the Russians than you were under the Germans. Perhaps it would be wise to leave Hungary and head for western Europe. Then again staying in Hungary might not be so bad if you could give up your Jewish identity.

If you leave Hungary for western Europe, turn to page 143.

If you stay, giving up your Jewish identity, turn to page 144.

92

With the help of the *Brichah* agents, you are able to cross the Hungarian border and enter Austria. Moving southward, you cross into Italy, breathing a sigh of relief. At Bari, you make contact with representatives of the *Haganah* and arrange to join this Jewish fighting force in the new State of Israel. Your days of active resistance to those who would kill Jews are not over.

A bushy gray-haired man walks into the meeting room. You recognize him immediately from his photographs. He is David Ben-Gurion. Almost by reflex, you spring to your feet in the presence of this great Zionist and Jewish leader.

Ben-Gurion tells your unit a terrifying story. The Syrians have purchased a huge quantity of military arms; if they are allowed to reach the Syrian army, it is possible that the Israelis will be defeated. The ship bearing these arms must be stopped.

Frogmen from your unit swim out to the Syrian ship, the Lino, and mine it. When the mines explode, the Lino sinks in Bari's harbor. The Syrians, however, are not so easily put off. They charter another ship, the Algiro, and reload it with weapons. But the harbor master is a friend of the Jews. He looks the other way and does not call the police when you and the others sneak aboard the Algiro and sail it out of the harbor, proudly flying the blue and white flag of Israel. When the ship enters Haifa harbor, you are all proclaimed heroes. The weapons that would have destroyed Israel can now protect Israel. "Operation Pirate" has been a huge success.

You decide that life on the sea suits you well. You apply for a commission in the Israeli navy. It is granted, and you become a naval officer, happy and proud to serve your people.

END

93

Having given most of your possessions and money to the government as required, you have very little left. Hopefully, there will be enough money to bribe the border guards and to pay for food, shelter, and transportation as you head south, having decided to use that southern land route. You travel from Hamburg to Munich and then cross the Austrian border at Salzburg. You move mostly at night to avoid the attention of the police and army patrols.

The farther you get from Berlin, the easier your journey becomes. From Austria, you cross into Italy and make your way to the port city of Trieste, where the Jewish community has established a hostel, giving temporary shelter to fugitives from Germany. Sheltered for a while, you think about your situation and consider what direction to take.

A representative from the *Jewish Agency for Palestine* suggests that you join a group trying to get into Palestine. The trip will be illegal, and the British will try to stop you from landing. However, he tells you how important it is for young people to get into the *Yishuv*.

You also meet Rabbi Joseph Schwarz during services in the hostel. He and his wife are also fleeing Germany and have decided to go by sea to the Philippine Islands. He invites you to join them. He believes that there will be no persecution of Jews in this Asian land.

If you decide to become part of the Yishuv, turn to page 161.

If you choose to go to the Philippines, turn to page 162.

94

The trip across the Atlantic is perilous; German subma-
rines have been known to torpedo even neutral ships. However, the three weeks of bouncing up and down end safely,
and you disembark at the Mexican port city of Veracruz.
Some of the cargo from the ship is being sent up to Mexico
City by truck, and you ride along, uncomfortably, on top of
the crates in the rear of the vehicle.

In Mexico City, you find the synagogue and enter just at
the time of *Minchah-Ma'ariv* prayers. When the services are
over, you introduce yourself to some of the worshipers. They
are astounded at your story. One of them offers you a room
at home, a good meal, a bath—all the things a free person
cherishes—and even the friendship of other free and safe
Jews.

You learn Spanish, make friends with other members of
the congregation and their families, and then decide, with
the help of one of your new friends, to get a job selling
clothing in a store owned by a member of the Jewish community.

You are so grateful that you volunteer to tutor young
children in Hebrew so that they can celebrate their *Bar/Bat
Mitzvah.* You become a welcome and respected member of
the Jewish community, and you live out the rest of your life
in great contentment.

END

95

Your heart pounds as you realize that you are truly free and that you are in the safest possible place in Europe for a Jew. The Swiss have maintained their neutrality during all recent European conflicts. No one will attack you as long as you remain here.

You turn to the synagogue and pray as you have never prayed before. All your gratitude and relief are concentrated in your daily recitals of the ancient words of the prayer book. You also begin to study with the rabbi, seeking to understand the secrets of the *Talmud* and the rabbinic *codes*. Both of you are astounded; you progress very quickly in your studies; it seems totally natural for you.

After five years of intensive study, you are brought before a "Bet Din," a rabbinic court, examined, and given rabbinic ordination. Your new colleagues then ask you to remain with them in Montreux and teach in their *yeshivah*. You agree. What more important task could you undertake than to teach survivors of the Holocaust to be Jews, to be proud, enthusiastic, and loyal Jews. This is what you do, living out your life with great satisfaction, certain that you are doing what God wants you to do.

END

96

Working in an automobile garage is really different. As a medical student in Berlin, clean hands were a must; now, as you learn to repair automobile engines, dirt under your fingernails is a mark of success. It takes you three years to graduate from apprentice to journeyman mechanic, and you are very proud of your accomplishment.

Three years is also the time it takes for the war to end. Now, you can travel freely throughout western Europe, but where? A representative of *ORT,* the *Organization for Rehabilitation through Training,* finds you in Spain and asks you to come to Paris to teach young refugees engine repair in the new *ORT* school. You like the idea of training a group of Jewish refugees and passing your new skill on to them; you accept.

Your students are often weak, still suffering from the rigors of concentration camps or their flight from the Nazis, but they are eager to learn. Many of them progress quickly, but, soon after graduation, they disappear. You wonder where they have gone. You later learn that they have been rushed to the new country of Israel and are among the mechanics for the new state's air force and army. You feel a tremendous sense of achievement. Your work has helped Jewish survival in a way you could never have imagined.

END

97

At Drancy, at least, conditions are a little better; there is air to breathe, and there is food. Your stay there, however, is brief. Within a few days, you and thousands of other Jews are packed onto a train. The door is locked shut; you are uncertain of the destination. There is nothing to do but save your energy for whatever comes; you try to find a place to rest. It's not easy because the Germans have put so many of you in the railroad car that you have no room even to sit down.

After a long ride, exhausted, hungry, bedraggled, you are finally let out of the car onto a long, concrete platform. Bright lights illuminate the night. Guards and barking attack dogs force you to move down the platform. If you do not move quickly enough, they hit you with clubs, yelling "schnell, schnell," hurry, hurry.

At the end of the platform, a German officer directs most of the trainload to one side with his baton; a few are shoved off to the other side. You notice that you are standing in a group of young men and women—no children, no old people, no sick people. You wonder what will happen to the rest. "They'll never be seen again," another prisoner tells you. "The Germans will kill them." But you have been selected to live.

You learn that you are at Auschwitz. Claiming that you are a watchmaker, you are assigned to that work.

Turn to page 146.

98

As your bus travels the short distance between Paris and Drancy, the driver is forced to slow up for a narrow bridge. As the bus leaves the bridge, you hear the sound of an explosion and see a bright flash. Suddenly, the bus lurches to the right and then falls over into a ditch. Because the guards are dazed, you are able to open the emergency door and quickly slip out.

Outside the bus, you are met by three men, in rough working clothes with blue berets, who look like farmers. They speak French, but you need to understand only one word: *Marquis.* They rush you away from the road and hide you until nightfall in a pit dug under a haystack.

Late at night, they come back with food and a change of clothing. The leader explains: "We can help you get into Switzerland where you will be safe. While it is not easy, we can make the arrangements." He also offers you another choice: "Join the resistance and fight the Germans."

If you choose to seek safety in Switzerland,
turn to page 147.

If you elect to join the resistance,
turn to page 148.

99

Mother Marie leads you to the Convent of the Little Cloister, a center of resistance activities which she and some priests have organized in Paris. For a few days, at least, you can stay here, hidden among the friendly nuns, well-fed and cared for. But you know that this is only a temporary refuge; you've got to find another place.

You approach Mother Marie with this problem, but she has already thought about it and has the solution. Among other documents she provides for you is a new identity card. "It is the card of a member of the Savigny family who was killed early in the war and whose baptism is recorded in this parish. The family is willing to have you stay with them. The Germans do not yet know of this death. You'll be safe."

However, you're afraid that too many neighbors will remember the members of the family, and one of them might give you away. The risk is very great.

*If you accept Mother Marie's solution,
turn to page 149.*

*If you decide to take the documents, but to
travel southward into the region of France
controlled by the pro-Nazi Vichy government,
turn to page 150.*

100

With the help of the "Oeuvres de Secours aux Enfants," an organization that helps children, you make contact with Robert Gamzon. This hero of the Jewish resistance has specialized in getting Jews into Switzerland and other countries where they will be safe from the Germans. A loose network of Jewish fighters is able to help you move from safe house to safe house, working your way southeast through France. Your major route is from Paris to the cathedral city of Orleans and then through the Loire Valley to Lyon.

You are hidden in the wine cellar of a famous restaurant in Lyon. During the day, you are relatively safe because few people come in to eat. At night, however, large numbers of German officers dine there, and at any moment one of them could insist on seeing the wine cellar. You and your hosts empty a large wine cask into which you can quickly crawl if you hear the door opening during the evening hours. In fact, you use this hiding place several times quite successfully.

Crossing the border into Switzerland has become too dangerous; the Germans are watching all the routes. Gamzon meets with you and suggests two alternatives: You can stay in Lyon, hidden in the home of a sympathetic Catholic widow, or, if you prefer, you can travel west, crossing through the forests of Correze into the province of Dordogne. In this area, the "Organization Juive de Combat," the Jewish Fighting Organization, can provide much better protection.

If you choose to remain hidden in Lyon, turn to page 151.

If you decide to travel west, turn to page 152.

101

Your loyalty to your friends means even more than protecting yourself, and you stay with them. This closeness helps you stay alive, and you feel less afraid of the future, knowing that you will share it with such good friends.

One day, the guards line up all the prisoners from your barracks. "You're going on a long trip," they laughingly taunt you. "You'll certainly see a lot of different scenery." A train of freight cars is backed up on the siding near the camp, and you are marched out under heavy guard. The guards count off eighty people for each car, force you in, and slam the doors shut. You hear the locks snap closed, and you feel trapped.

It seems like an eternity, but it is really only three days until you arrive at the Drancy camp near Paris. You are allowed to leave the train, stretch, and clean up. There are even a piece of dry bread and a bowl of watery soup for you to eat. You feel better, knowing that you are still in France and that the trip is over. The guards were surely teasing you; this wasn't as bad as you feared.

Turn to page 97.

102

It's a wrenching, difficult decision to leave your friends, but you know in your heart that the guard is right. By yourself, you have a much better chance to survive. Moving to another part of the camp, you do not get as involved in the lives of other inmates as before. Still, you feel like a traitor, leaving your friends and thinking only of yourself at a time when life has become so difficult.

What you are seeking is twofold: to escape from the camp and to get across the Pyrenees. If only you could reach Spain or Portugal, you would be safe.

Rumors had circulated in the camp that a "passeur" was active in the town of Lourdes, not far from the Gurs camp, helping Jewish fugitives across the Spanish border. Lourdes is the place where, Catholics believe, a young girl saw the image of the Virgin Mary. Catholics come to the site because of the healing power of its water. "Passing" from there into Spain will bring healing to you.

Your chance for escape comes during an intense rainstorm. Lightning and thunder combine with blinding rain, washing out part of the fence across from your barracks. You can hardly see, but you can't let this chance go by. You dash through the opening and out of the camp toward freedom. You stop for a moment, crouch behind a rock, and try to figure out in which direction to go to reach Lourdes.

If you go in an easterly direction, eventually arriving at Lourdes,
turn to page 154.

If you go in a northerly direction,
turn to page 153.

103

Keeping your eyes and ears open, you wander around the city. You soon discover that thousands of Jews are being hidden in Marseilles, in churches, in homes, and in factories. Throughout the city, patriotic French people are resisting the Germans by concealing Jewish refugees. You learn that a Capuchin monk, Father Marie-Benoit, is deeply involved in these illegal activities.

You go to the monastery on rue Croix de Rignier and explain your situation. Father Marie-Benoit extends his hand to you: "Come in, my child. We'll try to do something to make your life safer and easier." You discover that the monastery serves as a factory for false documents and identity papers. Soon, you have a new name, address, and personal history. You are someone else, at least on paper.

You volunteer to help Father Marie-Benoit and enthusiastically join in his work. However, the Vichy government is dissolved by the Germans who take direct control of southern France. Father Marie-Benoit moves to Milan, Italy, where he becomes known as Padre Benedette. Dressed as a monk, you go with him, helping him get hundreds of French Jews safely through the Alps.

When the Germans occupy Italy, you must make a choice. With your knowledge of German, you can work for the enemy as an interpreter. In reality, you would be acting as a spy; or, you can join and work with a resistance group.

If you decide to work for the Germans,
risking your life as a spy,
turn to page 155.

If you choose to work with the resistance,
turn to page 156.

104

The people who work on the docks of Marseilles are rough and sometimes violent, but they are honest according to their own code of ethics. Once they have decided to protect you, nothing can harm you. Even the German occupation troops are afraid to challenge their control of the dock area.

One day, one of your friends among the stevedores says: "Come with me. I've got something to show you." You walk along the wharves until you come to a small freighter, rusty and dilapidated. "This ship," he tells you, "is your ticket to freedom."

You look at the ship and cannot believe he is serious. The Martha Washington might be seaworthy in a bathtub, but not on the high seas. "Don't misjudge her," your friend tells you. "Since 1934, she has been making trips to North Africa every month, except that the North Africa she visits is spelled H-A-I-F-A! On this ship, you'll be able to get to Palestine."

Thanking him over and over, you race to gather your few possessions and board the ship, which is owned and operated by the *Jewish Agency*. To get past the British blockade, you are concealed in a box marked "Agricultural Equipment." Once you are ashore, you will be given a chance to decide what to do in Palestine.

If you go to the kibbutz of Ein Harod,
turn to page 157.

If you elect to join the Haganah,
turn to page 158.

Mr. Leyser, the store owner, treats you well. To him, you are like another member of the family, no different from his own daughter, Gerta. As he grows older, he arranges for you to purchase the store, and you suddenly find yourself a leading merchant in Collinsville, Illinois. You are well respected by the leading citizens of the city, and you spend a great deal of time trying to help them understand Jews and, especially, what has happened in Europe. You even bring the Midwest representative of the *Anti-Defamation League* to the Rotary Club meeting. He speaks about the strong bond between Jews and the new State of Israel. When you relate your own story on the Saint Louis, your non-Jewish friends begin to understand why Jews need a guaranteed refuge.

So, it is a great surprise to you when one of your non-Jewish friends tells you he has received an invitation from another business leader to join the local chapter of the *Ku Klux Klan.* The business leader tells your friend that the leading citizens of the city are signing up, trying to keep "those people" from taking over the town. You are shocked. You tell your friend to remind the person who issued the invitation that *Pastor Martin Niemoller* in Germany also thought discrimination against others was alright until, suddenly, it became an attack directly on him. Then, he realized that antagonism toward anyone can easily turn into hatred toward others—even self-hatred. However, you are alarmed by the overtones of prejudice in your own community.

If you stay in business in Collinsville,
turn to page 159.

If you choose to leave the city,
turn to page 160.

106

Your active participation in synagogue life at the Freilassing camp brings you great satisfaction. Making a *minyan* is
a real *mitzvah*. You are able to pray openly for the first time
since the war started.

One *Shabbat* afternoon, between *Minchah* and *Ma'ariv*
services, representatives from the *Agudat Yisrael* approach
you. "Listen!" they whisper to you. "All this talk about rees-
tablishing a Jewish state is sin and error. Only 'Mashiach,'
only the Messiah, has the right to rebuild Zion. If human
beings take over tasks which properly belong to God, terrible consequences will follow. Look what has happened to
the Jewish people because they did not stay faithful to God's
will."

They show you verses in the holy books which they
have interpreted as the basis for their ideas. They convince
you, and you abandon any plans you may have had to move
to Palestine.

You decide to go to America instead. When you settle
in New York, the *Agudat Yisrael* arranges for you to attend
Yeshiva University and then enter the medical school at
Mount Sinai Hospital. After completing your studies, you
marry and raise a family in a new home on Long Island.

You will never forget the advantages that the *Agudat
Yisrael* leadership made possible for you. Every day, you
drive to a Home for the Aged in Brooklyn and provide free
medical care for these elderly Jews. It's the least you can do
to help repay your debt of gratitude.

END

107

From Westerbork, you are sent to Auschwitz. The trip is a terrifying experience. Nearly 100 of you are crammed into a railway boxcar where some die of starvation before you even arrive at the camp. When the door is finally opened, you are pulled out and forced to march into the camp, under a gateway with a sign: "Arbeit Macht Frei," Work Leads to Freedom. The next morning, you and about 500 other Jews are put back on a train and sent to Berlin to work in the Krupp Munitions Factory.

Rumors reach you that the Nazis have made a mistake. Jews are rarely allowed out of that death camp. Somehow you and other Jews were included with a group of non-Jewish workers. You fully expect that they will return you to Auschwitz, but they do not; apparently, the officers are too embarrassed or afraid to admit their mistake.

In March 1945, the entire group is taken to Ravensbrück. Fortunately, within a month you are liberated and sent to Sweden to recuperate. Because you feel uncomfortable in Sweden, you decide to go back to Germany, to Nuremberg, where Nazis are being tried for their war crimes. You feel compelled to tell the world what they did, and you testify during the trials.

You live out the rest of your life in Germany, telling young Germans what happened during the Holocaust. You teach in a high school and feel satisfied that you are doing work that is important. Your work may prevent another anti-Semitic tragedy.

END

108

When you arrive at Bergen-Belsen, you are immediately put to work. Besides teaching Nazis how to cut diamonds, you are also required to cut many diamonds every day. You feel guilty because you know that your skill is helping the Germany army. Still, you must survive. You decide to cut the stones unevenly, hoping that this will make them less useful in the German war effort. Doing this makes you feel better. Despite the sabotage, you are skillful enough to continue through the war.

After the war, in 1946, you are among the first group of Jews emigrating to Palestine. From Germany, you travel by train, first to Lyon and then to Marseilles where you celebrate a *Pesach seder.* The SS Campollion takes you across the Mediterranean to Haifa. Then, after spending eight days at the transit camp in Athlit where all your processing is completed, you are allowed to leave. You return to Haifa and establish your own diamond cutting business. You decide to live the rest of your life there, practicing the skills which saved you from death in a concentration camp.

END

109

As an active leader of the camp council at Freilassing, you serve the camp well. However, camp conditions are still awful; you feel you must do as much as you can to improve them. When Dr. Zalman Grunberg calls together camp representatives from nearly all the camps, except Bergen-Belsen and a few small ones, at St. Ottilien, a hospital camp just north of Munich, you join him. Together with the other representatives, you compose a declaration, demanding that the Allied armies improve camp conditions, give preference to Jewish refugees who endured a special horror under the Nazis, and permit Jews to make *aliyah* to Palestine.

A press conference is called. You and the other representatives read the proclamation aloud in the Munich beer hall which had been the early headquarters of Hitler's *Brownshirts.* You sense an extra thrill at being able to speak about the Jewish future in this room where the death of the Jewish people was so avidly plotted during the years before Hitler came to power. As you and the others hold the Torah high, you sing aloud: "Am Yisrael Chai," The People Israel Lives.

You have never been prouder than at this moment. A terrible price has been exacted from your people, but you have survived. Never again will you and others allow such a tragedy to happen. You spend the rest of your life helping Jewish refugees become proud and strong defenders of the Jewish future. It is a task to which you gladly dedicate your life.

END

110

Although you stay with the Catholic widow in Lyon, you make it very clear to her that you are proud and glad to be Jewish. She understands and even occasionally goes to the synagogue with you.

What she does not know is that you are part of a secret group in regular contact with Simon Wiesenthal. You are particularly interested in tracing a Nazi officer known as the "Butcher of Lyon," Klaus Barbie, who has tricked the American army into letting him escape justice. You and your colleagues in Lyon send letters, make telephone calls, and even take trips to find Barbie. His acts against Jews and members of the resistance were so atrocious that he must be brought to trial and punished.

You pursue him for almost forty years. Finally, in 1984, Barbie is arrested in Paraguay and returned to prison in France. You are at the airport when he arrives. With his wrists chained, he is rushed into a police van and taken to the same prison he once commanded.

You have a strange feeling of emptiness. The hunt is now over. You had thought you would feel vengeful, perhaps would want to kill Barbie yourself. But you no longer feel that way. He is a pitiful old man, hardly the superman of Nazi legend. You realize that you, a Jew, and all decent people have won.

END

111

"Address!" the clerk shrieks out at you, as you stand at attention before her. "Gartnerstrasse," you mumble, all your pride from last night gone in an agony of dread. But, when you glance down, you notice that she has made an error. Instead of writing "Gartnerstrasse" on the address line, she has put "Gartner" in the occupation space. You think about correcting her, but then you think again. Nobody corrects the *SS*.

One fine, spring day, you stop to pick a few straggly wild flowers near the barbed wire fence. The guards grab you, but you tell them that the flowers are for an officer. The officer is amused by your gesture and looks up your file. When he finds that you are listed as a "Gartner," a gardener, he assigns you to the officers' garden. You really don't know what you are doing, but you manage. After all, these working conditions are much better than those elsewhere, and you can even sneak a little extra food to eat.

After the war, you apply for admission to the United States. The new Wiley-Revercomb Immigration Act favors agricultural workers. Through the *Gestapo*'s error, you qualify for this special consideration. The Jewish community of Pasadena, California, arranges to sponsor you, and you find yourself there in December, stuffing flowers into the wire frame of a Rose Bowl parade float.

You think to yourself: "I did not survive the horrors of Dachau to put flowers on a parade float. There must be more." And, of course, there is. You enroll at the Hebrew Union College-Jewish Institute of Religion and train to become a rabbi. When you are ordained, you are certain that your survival has been justified.

END

112

The stench of the crematoria rises in your nostrils as you work on the burial detail. Dead people are thrown into mass graves; sick people are sometimes burned alive. Your stomach is constantly knotted and churning with the horror of what you are doing, but you have no choice. It's this or death. So, you go on, working like an animal, slowly starving to death yourself on 500 calories a day.

When you return from each day's work, you and the other *Sonderkommando* members form a *minyan* in your barracks to say "Kaddish." It's illegal, but it's the only thing that helps you keep your sanity. It's certainly the least you can do for those pitiful dead people.

Most *Sonderkommando* members are killed after about a month to eliminate witnesses, but the rapid Allied advance alters the Nazis plans. On May 18, 1945, you are driven out of the camp on a forced march, just a few miles ahead of the advancing Allied army. At night, you are locked in a barn, and you fear the worst. But nothing happens. In the morning, you hear the rumble of a tank. It bears a strange red, white, and blue flag as it grinds to a halt in front of the barn. Its turret turns slowly; then the hatch opens. A huge man descends, and you are petrified. You have never seen a black man before. But he and his friends are kind. They give you their own food and help you to find shelter at one of the new Displaced Persons camps in the area.

If you go to the camp at Feldafing,
turn to page 163.

If the camp at Windsheim is nearer, and you
go there,
turn to page 164.

113

When you arrive in Ravensbrück, you are nearly dead from the horrid conditions in the cattle cars. Many others have, in fact, died. But you remember the example of Rabbi Baeck, and you are determined to survive.

You are assigned to the Malchow-Mecklenburg factory where you spend twelve hours each day making artillery shells for the German army. It saddens you to know that these munitions will be used to kill good people. You feel like a traitor; you do not know how to stop without being killed.

Some of the others in the underground bunkers where you work understand how you feel; they have the same attitude. Together, you find ways to sabotage the weapons —putting too little gunpowder in the shells, bending the timing devices, and making other tiny changes that will prevent the shells from striking their targets accurately. If you are caught, you will be shot, but the risk is worthwhile. It is your way of resisting the enemy, of fighting back. You are doing your share to help defeat Hitler.

When Germany surrenders, you are taken to the Displaced Persons camp at Landsberg. There you learn to forge ration cards for Jewish survivors to get badly needed extra food. Later, you move to Buenos Aires, Argentina, where you establish an engraving business. You help found a congregation with many fellow survivors. The name you select for your congregation is important to you: "Lamrot Hakol," In Spite of Everything. You will always remain a faithful Jew.

END

114

Nothing that has happened to you makes any sense. Civilized people do not try to exterminate an entire society, a complete culture. You cannot understand what is going on. All you know is that your well-ordered, sensible life has been turned upside-down.

When you arrive at Dachau, the confusion continues. You are processed like any other prisoner, stripped of your clothing and given filthy rags to wear, assigned to an overcrowded barrack, issued a bowl and a spoon, and fed a watery soup. Your head is shaved and a number tattooed onto your left forearm. You feel that you have landed on a different planet.

Just as unexpectedly, however, you are called into the central office, where an officer informs you that there must have been a terrible error. You have been imprisoned by mistake and are now free to go. Absolutely no explanation is given. You do not understand why this is happening to you; you have never heard of any prisoner being released like this. However, you do not ask questions, fearing the authorities will change their minds again.

Once outside the gates, with new identification cards and some money given you by the sympathetic camp commander, you try to decide which way to go.

Switzerland, which is close by, will be safe. However, it will be difficult to cross the border. Perhaps France would be a more suitable destination.

*If you decide to go to Switzerland,
turn to page 147.*

*If you elect to go to France,
turn to page 167.*

115

You cross back over the Öresund, this time in safety and in broad daylight, landing in the small city of Helsingör (Elsinore). As soon as you step off the boat, you see the famous castle depicted in Shakespeare's play, "Hamlet." This is a wonderful country with generous, kind people, and you decide to settle right here in Helsingör.

You finish your medical training and become a physician. Remembering the Jewish aged you left behind and who were taken to Theresienstadt, you specialize in helping the older members of the community. They and their families deeply appreciate what you are able to do for them, and you spend the rest of your life as a respected and loved member of the community.

When you retire, you have only one regret: You have lost contact with the Jewish community and with the Jewish religion. Perhaps, you think, you could go back. But it is too late. The Danes saved your life, but the war stole your religion.

END

116

You look at the globe. To you, the farthest place from Sweden appears to be Australia, and you make arrangements to go there. You don't know anyone there, but it's a new life, far distant from Europe and far from all those unbearable memories.

The ship takes you to Perth, a city on the west coast of the continent. There, you go to an employment service to see what jobs are available. The only employment they can offer you is as a sheep herder at a ranch in the Outback. You accept. What choice do you have, new in the country and without any money?

Once on the ranch, you find that this new life suits you well. You impress your employer with your intelligence and willingness to work hard. He is an older man who teaches you all the aspects of the ranching business. When he dies, you discover that he has willed the entire ranch to you. You are now a prosperous ranch owner with large tracts of land, thousands of sheep, and dozens of people working for you.

Your ranch is far from Perth, but you make the trip into the city every month. Your ranch hands think you are going on business, but that is only partly true. You always stop at the synagogue to say two prayers: the "Kaddish" in memory of your European family who perished during the Holocaust and the "Shehecheyanu" in thanks to God for your good fortune in your adopted country.

END

117

The Allied bombers have reduced large neighborhoods of the city to rubble, and many Germans have found that the only way for them to manage is to dig caves under the debris. You and others who have chosen this way of life survive by digging through garbage cans to find whatever you can to eat, clothe yourselves, and heat your pitiful shelters.

One day, as you are making your rounds through the back alleys of Berlin, reeking from garbage, hungry, clad in rags, you are stopped by the police. They examine your stolen identity papers and conclude that you cannot be the person described on them. You try to explain that the life you have been leading has changed your appearance, that the picture is really you, the way you used to look. They don't believe you. They take you to police headquarters, where you are eventually identified as a Jew.

You are placed on a prison train and sent south to the concentration camp at Dachau.

Turn to page 66.

118

With six other friends, some fugitive Jews and some *Aryan* Germans, you live in a one-room apartment. The landlord seems to be decent enough, but you make sure he receives extra money every month to assure his silence. With the help of Christian friends on the outside, you get a job as a tailor in a clothing factory.

You use some of your hard-earned money to buy a pistol and a hand grenade on the black market. You keep these in your coat pockets in case a *Gestapo* agent ever tries to arrest you. "If they want me," you think to yourself, "they will have to die with me!" You have some close calls, but you never have to use these weapons.

One day, a high-ranking German officer comes into the factory and orders a civilian suit. You wonder why he would do that. You are especially intrigued when he leaves his fancy uniform behind, walking out of the shop dressed in his new clothing. "Can it be," you wonder, "that the end of the *Third Reich* is near, that this officer is trying to conceal his identity and sneak away before the Allies get to Berlin?"

You're sure that is the answer. Quickly, you gather up his uniform and put it on. You march out and order a staff car to drive you toward the western front. When you are close to the fighting, you walk into the woods, strip off the uniform, and make your way toward the British army units in front of you. You raise your hands over your head so they don't shoot you; you are soon in the custody of His Majesty's soldiers.

Turn to page 168.

119

The good minister has played a little joke on you. Not only did he find you a job in a cemetery in Weissensee, but even in a Jewish cemetery! You are responsible for keeping the grass cut and the weeds down, but there are no new graves to dig. You live in an old mausoleum, and, while it is cold in winter, you manage without great difficulty. The *SS* is strangely superstitious and will not enter a cemetery; everyone else seems to leave you alone, thinking you odd, but harmless.

In April 1945, the Russian army captures that part of Berlin in which you are living. A squad of soldiers pushes you against the wall and prepares to shoot you. You know only one word of Russian, and you shout it out: "Zhid, Zhid," Jew, Jew. The Russian sergeant doesn't believe you. "We know that the Germans killed all the Jews in Germany. You're lying." But you strip off your coat and reveal the yellow star you were forced to wear, now sewed to your undershirt. Finally, the Russians believe you and let you go.

You settle in East Berlin and try to make a new life for yourself. But, one day, you overhear two men in a cafe: "Damned Jews are returning. I thought we'd finally gotten rid of those lice."

This bitter reminder of anti-Semitism is too much for you to bear. You cross over into the Allied zone of West Germany, eventually making your way to Israel. You will never again live in a country where Jews can be slandered or attacked in this way.

END

120

The Siemens Munitions Factory near Berlin makes much of the ammunition for the German army. You are assigned the dangerous work of rolling huge barrels of gunpowder from one building to another. One wrong move, and you could be blown up in an instant. Every so often, there are explosions, where workers are killed or injured; but you are very careful and avoid accidents.

You notice that some of the laborers are Jews, brought from the nearby concentration camps. They are always given the worst jobs, treated miserably, and fed practically nothing. It pains you to watch them waste away before your eyes, and you invent little ways to ease their lot. If you are caught, you'll be executed, but you could not live with yourself if you did not do something, pass them a piece of bread, help lift a heavy load, something.

When the war ends, you present yourself to the American army's Judge Advocate General's office and testify about the worst of the Nazi supervisors in the factory. On the basis of your testimony, a number of them are arrested, tried for war crimes, and sent to prison. It makes you feel better that some justice has been served.

Several years later, you get to America where you decide to become a lawyer. Bringing justice to the world—as the Bible says: "Justice, justice shall you pursue"—is an old Jewish idea. You want to be part of that idea. You commit your life to the pursuit of justice and fairness.

END

121

A new organization, the Committee for the Assistance of Jewish Refugees, is established. This time, the refugees themselves will decide what is to be done. You do not feel as angry at Victor Sassoon, Silas Hardoon, and the other *Sephardim* as some of the people, but you understand their desire to have a say in their own future; therefore, you join with them.

With few relief funds coming in from outside the community, survival is often desperate. You must scrounge, beg, borrow, and plead for any help you can find. You and the others try to help everyone, but you pay particular attention to the needs of widows and orphans. "After all," you say, "if we cannot remain faithful to the biblical *mitzvot,* we really won't be Jews very much longer."

Somehow, everyone manages, although not easily. The relief situation improves in 1944 when the United States allows Jewish organizations to send money to China; it becomes even easier when the *Nationalists* under Chiang Kai-shek drive the Japanese out of China. You cannot believe that you have survived the war, but it is true. You stop at the synagogue to *bench gomel* for your safe passage through this terrible time. However, you feel that it would be in your best interests to leave Shanghai with its memories of difficult times and start a new life elsewhere. You decide to go to Indonesia.

Turn to page 169.

122

With your training at medical school, you are hired as a teacher of biology at the Kadoorie School in Shanghai. You enjoy working with the young Jewish students and even volunteer to help coach a soccer team. As the boys and girls get to know you better, they confide in you, telling you their secret hopes, fears, and doubts. You are glad to help them by listening sympathetically.

After the school day, you usually read a Shanghai *Yiddish* newspaper called "Unser Leben," Our Life, and, occasionally, you go to the *Yiddish* theater. You also do part-time volunteer work for the Shanghai Jewish Youth Association on Kinchow Road, and it is this experience which points you toward a new career.

When the war ends, you emigrate to the United States where you find a job with the Jewish Community Center in Los Angeles. There, you work as a youth leader until you retire. You are not a wealthy person, but you are content; you feel that contributing to the future generation of Jewish life has made your life worthwhile.

E N D

123

The Mir *Yeshivah* establishes itself again in Jerusalem. You continue your talmudic studies until you have reached a high level of knowledge. Three rabbis test your understanding and, when you pass their examination, you are granted the rabbinical title of "Morenu Harav." You think back to the days when you were studying medicine in Berlin, and you cannot believe that you spent so many years in secular studies when you should have been studying the sacred books of the Jewish people from early childhood. "Judaism can only survive," you conclude, "if we remain true to our Torah. Ignorance and the violation of our holy tradition can only result in misfortune for the Jews. God expects us to return to what we are supposed to do—study and teach Torah. That is true Judaism."

Every evening, you walk to the King David Hotel. From there you can see the only part of the ancient Temple that remains standing, the Western Wall. You cannot approach any closer because that part of Jerusalem is occupied by Jordanian soldiers. You pray that God will one day allow you the privilege of worshiping at the Wall so that you will fulfil the destiny of all Jews to return to the holy mountain of the Temple and bring the Messiah down to earth. "Ken yehi ratson," you chant, "Thus may it be God's will."

END

124

From the day you arrived in Brooklyn, your world has been confused and troubled. Nothing seems right to you. Finally, you ask for an audience with the *Rebbe,* and you try to explain your problem. "My child," this holy man responds, "you are trying to do too much. What *Hashem* wants from you is a simple life. Marry, raise a large family, study the holy books. That will be enough."

You follow the *Rebbe*'s advice, and it seems to work. Your mind is now at ease, and all your troubles appear to be in the past.

All your troubles—except your relationship with another group of *Chasidim* who live nearby in Williamsburg. These *Chasidim* are opposed to the creation of the State of Israel. "Only the Messiah may reestablish Zion," they claim. "The Zionists are taking over what the Messiah alone can do. It is a sin, and it is doomed to failure."

You and the other people of the Mir *Yeshivah* respond angrily. "Maybe God wants us to act now," you scream out. "Besides, we have family at the *yeshivah* in Jerusalem. Without Israel, they would be slaughtered by the Arabs. Israel must live." But you cannot convince your opponents, and the two groups continue to live with bitter antagonism.

Despite the problems which still exist, following the *Rebbe*'s advice has been a good decision. Your life is stable and productive. With your spouse and six children, you live out your life as a secure member of a fine Jewish community.

END

125

You present yourself at the Ministry of Foreign Affairs and fill out the numerous forms that are required for an exit permit, applying for "family reunion" status to join your cousin, your only living relative, in Melbourne, Australia.

After a delay of six months, you are ordered back to the ministry and informed that permission to leave has been granted. However, you must surrender your Russian citizenship, your medal, and most of your possessions and money. You are left with only enough money to reach Australia.

After arduous travel over land and sea from Vilna, seeing parts of the world you had read about only in geography books—Odessa, the Black Sea, deserts in Arabia, steaming cities in India, beautiful islands—eventually you board a cargo ship for the last lap of your journey. For weeks you bounce across the Indian Ocean, finally docking in Melbourne.

With your cousin, you try to settle into this new country, but, at first, you are not comfortable here. One *Shabbat* morning, as you sit in the synagogue, however, you close your eyes during the rabbi's sermon and think: "To be a Jew is like being a member of a family; family is the most important thing." At that moment, you realize that you will be happy as long as you have your Jewish family with you.

END

126

With your knapsack and walking stick, you set out to walk to Israel. Heading south, you pass the Russian cities of Minsk and Zhitomir. After a very long and tiring trip, you pass through the city of Kishinev, where, sixty years before, terrible pogroms ravaged the Jewish residents. During a dark night, you pay a boatman to take you across the Dniester River to Roumania.

Because Roumania has good relations with Israel, it is not difficult to arrange passage on a boat from that country to the Israeli port of Haifa. Haifa is beautiful, but you are not satisfied. Every day in your prayers, you have asked God for the privilege of seeing Jerusalem. That is where you must live.

After reaching and settling in Jerusalem, you begin to tour the city. When you arrive at *Yad Vashem*, you walk slowly through the building. Later, with tears streaming down your face, you sit on a bench among the trees honoring Righteous Gentiles, non-Jews who risked their lives to save Jews. You realize that the Jewish world remembers what you and other resisters have done; your life is honored by this memorial, and even the loss of your leg seems less important.

You retire in Israel with a pension provided by the government and with an inner sense of satisfaction and self-respect.

END

127

It's only a short distance up the Danube River to Bratislava. At night you walk across the border into Czechoslovakia. When you reach Marchegg, *Brichah* agents help you cross a teetering wooden bridge into Austria. You never learn about the bribes and other devices that *Brichah* used to make your trip possible, but you are deeply grateful.

With their help, you journey across Austria to Salzburg, home of Wolfgang Amadeus Mozart, a beautiful city high in the Austrian Alps. To get beyond Salzburg, however, is not easy. The border with Germany has been sealed shut by the American army, partly to keep former Nazi leaders from escaping as refugees. You cannot understand why you are prevented from going ahead. "I'm not a Nazi," you argue. "Anyone can see that. Why should I be punished for what those criminals have done?"

An American army captain, Stanley K. Novinsky, hears your complaint. He is not a Jew; in fact, he comes from a Polish-American Catholic family. However, aware of what has happened to the Jews in Europe, he feels your pain deeply and quietly arranges for your safe passage. Soon, you are able to enter the Displaced Persons camp at Freilassing in southern Germany. Although conditions are not good, you are at least safe and among friends for the first time in many years. Wanting to express your gratitude by serving the camp in some useful capacity, you look into the opportunities open to you.

If you serve as a camp council leader,
turn to page 109.

If you become active in the camp synagogue,
turn to page 106.

128

In the Displaced Persons camp where you have gone after the French liberation, you receive a letter from a relative in Los Angeles, inviting you to settle there and become a partner in his construction business. It takes nearly two years to get all your papers in order—health records, police reports, visas, and immigration documents. Finally, you are permitted to travel to America and on to Los Angeles where your relative meets you.

The demand for housing after World War II is great, especially in the booming region of Southern California. You and your relative specialize in building small, inexpensive homes. They are sold quickly, and you make a great deal of money, more than you ever dreamed of and more than you would ever need for yourself.

As you read through the *machzor* on a *Yom Kippur* afternoon, you notice a quotation from *Pirke Avot:* "Who is a hero? One who makes peace with his neighbor." This gives you an idea. You remember the kindness of the Catholics in Lyon and decide to create a center for interfaith activities, a community center in which all people will be welcome.

It is a proud day when the new community center is dedicated. At the mayor's invitation, you attend the ceremony in Lyon. He tells you that your gift will build a place of peace and understanding. You are proud of your decision, and you feel that you may have taken a small step toward preventing any future Holocaust.

END

129

You succeed in contacting the *Brichah* organization. *Brichah* gets you out of Poland, across Czechoslovakia, and into Austria. There you are loaded onto military-looking trucks, identified with the words: "Hq, US Forces, French Zone, Austria." A Turkish Jew named Sami Levi, who serves with the *Haganah,* drives you across Austria, southward through Italy, and into the port city of Bari. From there, the *Aliyah Bet* people smuggle you aboard a ship to Palestine.

You settle on top of Mount Carmel in Haifa and begin to put your life back into order. One of your greatest pleasures is to take a leisurely stroll on *Shabbat* afternoon, walking by the Bahai Temple and through the tree-lined streets. On one such walk, you pass a Carmelite monk who looks familiar. Five steps farther on, you whirl around. "Sir, I know you from somewhere. Wait a minute! Weren't you once known as Oswald?"

He recognizes you as well. He tells you that he survived the war because Jewish partisans prevented Russian soldiers from executing him. After the war, he converted to Catholicism and came to Palestine to be a monk at the monastery in Haifa. He is now known as Brother Daniel and has appealed to the government for citizenship. He still thinks of himself as a Jew, at least in part.

You shake hands and leave. You are sad that he chose a path different from yours, conversion, leaving Judaism behind. You are glad that you have remained a Jew; it gives you pride and satisfaction.

END

130

With memories of Treblinka fresh in your mind—particularly those memories of new inmates brought to the camp after the uprising in Warsaw—you head south on your improbable trip. You do not take the most direct route but decide to circle around the areas of heaviest German concentration. You head first for Yugoslavia, then for northern Italy, where you recall hearing that there are partisan groups to help you.

Indeed they do. With a lot of assistance, hard work, and patience, you are able to reach the southern shore of Lac Leman, just east of Geneva, Switzerland. Grateful that your father *taught you how to swim,* you slip into the cold water and paddle the last few miles into the safety of Swiss neutrality.

When you reach Geneva, you seek out *Gerhart Riegner* to tell him your story. He tries to communicate the facts to the Allies, but no one believes him. You feel that your efforts have been in vain and pledge that you will not rest until you make the world understand what the Nazis are doing to the Jewish people. You owe a debt to those who are being murdered, and you swear you will not rest until that debt is paid.

Many years later, having survived the war, you attend the opening of *Yad Vashem* outside Jerusalem. Tears run down your face as you walk through the building and stand in front of the eternal flame. Although the recollection of what happened in Europe is still bitter in your soul, a heavy weight has been lifted from your heart. Now that *Yad Vashem* exists, you are satisfied that your story will be told, and the world will know. You have fulfilled your oath, and you are free.

E N D

131

It takes nearly a month, but you finally link up with a partisan unit near Minsk. In fact, it is a Jewish unit led by Hersh Smoliar and Misha Gildenman, and you are immensely grateful to have discovered such a courageous band of modern *Maccabees*.

The conditions in the camp are hardly luxurious. It is almost always cold and wet, and there is rarely enough food. Most of the time, you are either hiding or fleeing, and there is always a gnawing fear that you will be caught. But positive rewards also exist. The disruption of German trains when you blow up the tracks means that the war is being slowed down, that the death camps are not operating as easily, and that people are being saved. You feel that you are fulfilling the wisdom of the *Talmud*: "*If one saves a single life, it is considered as if one has saved the entire world*."

Although you feel good having saved some Jews from extermination, you know how many tens of thousands you could not help. The guilt you feel at this failure haunts you long after the war; you cannot shake it off. "Why did I survive?" you wonder. "Why did they have to die? Why couldn't I save them, too?"

You spend many years in treatment with a psychiatrist who specializes in working with people who feel such guilt. However, your treatment is unsuccessful and, finally, you are admitted to a hospital where you will live as a patient until you die.

END

132

At the Cinecitta refugee camp near Rome, your language skills are recognized; your special talent sets you apart from others. Because of this, you are selected for training as an airline ticket agent, someone who will have contact with international travelers and who can help them in their own language.

When you graduate from the training program, your supervisor shows you your progress report. You are stunned. He has written that it is acceptable for you to be in close contact with customers because you "do not look obviously Jewish." You cannot believe what you are reading. Here, even in a training program for Jews, you find anti-Semitism. Impossible, but true!

You conclude that trying to be a Jew in the *Diaspora* has been a terrible mistake. You make immediate plans to continue your travels to Israel as soon as the state becomes independent. When you arrive, you settle in Tel Aviv and become one of the first employees of the new Israeli airline, El Al. Your training pays off; you have a career of which you can be proud. Here, in a Jewish country, you will not encounter the anti-Jewish problems of the *Diaspora*. Here, you are accepted; here, you belong. It's a wonderful feeling.

END

133

After a long and tiring trip, you arrive in Mobile where your sponsor helps you find a job in a hardware store and a place to live. You begin to learn the hardware business, how to use the cash register, and how to deal with the customers. Inside the store, all goes well.

Outside the store, however, you are astonished by the treatment of black people. Blacks are not permitted to use the same bathrooms, benches, water fountains, restaurants, and hotels as whites. What makes you even angrier is that some southern Jews accept this segregation. When you try to explain to them that this form of racism is but one step removed from Nazism and its racial hatred of the Jews, they reject the comparison. They tell you to keep your opinions to yourself. "Don't rock the boat!"

However, you continue voicing your opinions. You have learned the hard way that discrimination against one can lead very quickly to discrimination against others. What happens to blacks can happen to Jews. You speak out, finding few white allies but many enemies. Sometimes, they throw garbage on your lawn and bricks through your windows, but you persist. What is right is right!

When Reverend Martin Luther King, Jr., comes to Mobile, he meets you and thanks you for your efforts. There is something spiritual and forceful about this black leader; if he believes in you, you will have the strength to continue your lonely fight. Other members of the Jewish community join your work, and you are encouraged. "In America," you say to yourself, "justice will eventually win."

END

134

The owner of the store explains the policy of "dhimmi," the second-class rights of tolerated non-Moslems. Islamic law requires that infidels who sell items to Moslems stand below them. "These pits help us to stay out of conflict with the law. After all, as Jews we know that compromises are necessary if we are to be safe here."

Jews! Here! You have found the answer. The owner tells you that, in Teheran, there is a Jewish orphanage run by the local Jewish community and by representatives from the *Jewish Agency for Palestine.* You race back to your group and tell them this wonderful news.

The next day, you and the other adults gather the children together for a hike. You tell the Polish priest that you are helping keep them fit for future army service, and he agrees that this is a good idea. As soon as you are away from the Polish camp, however, you head directly for the orphanage, where you are greeted by Meir Ohad and Tsiporah Sharrett. When you tell them your story, they gladly accept the children into the orphanage.

Several months later, you join a caravan that crosses northern Iraq and Syria, descending through Lebanon into Palestine. You feel that you are reliving history for this is the same route that the Jews took when they returned to the Holy Land after the Babylonian Exile, 2,500 years ago. Once you arrive in Palestine, you take the children to the youth village at Ben-Shemen.

Your work with the children has been rewarding. You feel you have helped improve the world and decide to continue in that line of work. You get a job at Ben-Shemen and remain there, helping refugee children live better lives.

END

135

The time you spent traveling across southern Russia with the children, living among the religious Jews of that region, affected you greatly. Religion, which had previously not been important to you, is now your major interest. The power of Judaism has become the major force in your life.

When you reach the holy city of Jerusalem, you enter the very Orthodox section called "Mea Shearim" and enroll in one of the many Orthodox *yeshivot* which are located there. During the next few years, you study and think. You come to believe that another Holocaust will never happen if Jews remain faithful to their covenant with *Hashem*. Every *Yom Kippur* when you pray "Ashamnu, bagadnu," We have sinned and we have rebelled, your heart is filled with sadness. The penalty for disobedience was heavy, the price high, but you have learned the lesson: The only way to protect the Jewish people is loyalty to the Torah and the commandments.

The people at your *yeshivah* already agree with you, and you decide that the greatest *mitzvah* is to persuade non-observant Jews to change their ways. You and a few others establish a new school called the *Diaspora Yeshivah* and search for students who will return to traditional Jewish ways. Many Jewish young people from all over the world study in your school, and you feel a great sense of satisfaction because you are sure that you are carrying out the will of *Hashem*.

END

136

With the children settled in the camp at Athlit, you now try to decide what you will do. Since you were a small child, you have been hearing about the *chalutzim* who settled on kibbutz settlements, who drained the Huleh marshes and swamps, and who made the brown, dry Negev flower as it had in the days of the ancient Nabataeans. This productive life appeals to you, and you make arrangements to join the kibbutz at Sde Boker.

There, you spend your days helping grow cotton, a new crop which will be sold overseas, bringing badly-needed money to the new state. The agricultural work is hard but rewarding. Your most treasured experiences come when the most famous son of the kibbutz, David Ben-Gurion, returns for a few days of rest and conversation. He radiates excitement and dedication to the *Zionist* task, and you always leave his presence inspired. Whatever problems you face seem small compared to his worries, and he gives you confidence to meet every crisis and solve it.

One *Pesach,* when you and your family attend the *seder,* you are called upon to recite some of the prayers. "Baruch Atah Adonai Elohenu Melech ha'olam shehecheyanu. . . ." You sing the praises of God for keeping you alive and allowing you to reach this festive day. Then you begin to laugh.

"When I first came here," you explain, "I couldn't believe in God. After all that happened in Europe, how could anyone pray to a God who would allow those terrible events? But now I understand. I look around at my family and friends and my good life here. God has, indeed, been good to me!"

END

137

The march continues for several weeks, leaving a trail of dead and dying Jews across the landscape. There are no medical supplies, and you are not permitted to use your training to make even the most painfully ill of your companions more comfortable. As you watch people die, one by one, you become bitterly angry, but there is nothing you can do; you are helpless and frustrated.

One morning, the *SS* guards force all of you to lie face down in a ditch at the side of the road. You are sure that the crackle of machine gun fire will soon be heard, that you will be massacred, as so many other Jews have been. However, nothing happens. After a long wait, you have the courage to turn your head; you are surprised that the guards are gone. They have all disappeared, fleeing for their own lives!

You and the other survivors drag yourselves into a nearby village where horrified people try to help you. They give you food and shelter and make you as comfortable as they can. The warm barn where these kind folks have sheltered you seems like a palace, compared to what you have been through.

When the Allied soldiers enter the town, they, too, try to help. Each of you is interviewed and allowed to make a decision about where you want to go.

If you choose to continue toward western Europe, not wishing to return to Poland, turn to page 165.

If you decide to go back, seeking any survivors in your family, turn to page 166.

138

A cantor who used to be the chazan in the Great Synagogue of Pest has organized a choir in Buchenwald. You find it strange and eerie to hear beautiful music in the midst of such tragedy, but the German officers enjoy the entertainment. You look upon the singing as a way to keep yourself alive.

On April 11, 1945—a day you will never forget—American soldiers liberate Buchenwald and its few remaining inmates. These are the first Americans you have ever met. They overflow with kindness, doing everything they can to help you. They give you a chocolate bar which you eat so quickly that you become ill; you are not used to so many calories at once. But gradually you adjust to your life as a free person.

Some time later, you get the opportunity to go to America where you live in Brooklyn, New York. There you work in a small clothing business and join a small synagogue. Everytime you hear the chazan or look at the *Shabbat* candles, you see the ghosts of people you knew in Buchenwald. You know that someday you must return.

Year-after-year, you save your money until you have enough for a journey back to Buchenwald. You reenter this camp of horrors and find the place where your barracks were located. Quietly, to yourself, you sing *El Male Rachamim* and then recite the "Kaddish."

With tears in your eyes, you know that you will never forget.

END

139

As soon as you enter the hospital, you know something very strange is happening there. No one seems to be trying to cure the patients; no one relieves their suffering. Soon, you discover the truth.

Dr. Hans Eysele is in charge. However, he is not interested in medicine. He is interested only in research to prove that *Aryans* are superior to Jews. He is conducting experiments on the mentally retarded and on twins, experiments that leave nearly all his patients dead.

You wish you could be elsewhere, but you have no choice. Thus you decide to observe, making a mental record of everything you see, so that, should you survive, you can tell about these horrors to the world.

In April 1945, as the American army advances toward Buchenwald, the order is given to shoot all witnesses to the medical experiments. However, the guards fear that the Americans will kill them if they continue shooting innocent Jews. During the commotion that follows, you slip back into the general camp population. The momentary lapse of German discipline helps you survive.

Years later, having gone to America, you find a new career, working for the Jewish Family and Children's Service in a large American city. Most of your work involves helping refugees make new homes for themselves. Soviet Jews, Vietnamese, Cubans, and many others begin new lives with your assistance. Perhaps all the suffering you endured made you better able to perform these *mitzvot.*

END

140

When you leave Budapest, you head east toward the Ukraine where the Jewish partisan units have been most effective in fighting the Germans. You feel you must ally yourself with one of these groups because you are tired of letting the Germans have their way. You feel it is time to resist more actively. You also know that you will feel comfortable only among other Jews. One unhappy lesson you have learned in the last few years is that you cannot trust the non-Jews who live in Eastern Europe. Their anti-Semitism is sometimes so strong that, although they hate the Germans, they would rather turn you over to them than enlist your support to fight them.

As you move farther east, past the cities of Berdichev and Zhitomir, famous Jewish communities of the past, you recall a name you once heard: Abba Kovner. Somewhere someone told you that he was a courageous commander of a resistance unit near Kiev. Kovner is the leader you must find.

Your trip covers over five hundred miles, much of it through areas heavily patrolled by the Germany army. Several times, you have narrow escapes. Once, German soldiers even begin a conversation with you, but they think you are only a local peasant. You are able to keep your real identity hidden. After two months of travel, almost all of it on foot, you reach the camp where the Jewish resistance movement has its center.

Turn to page 43.

141

A wave of excitement runs through you as you make your decision. For years, you have said "Hashanah haba'ah Birushalayim," Next year in Jerusalem, at the *Pesach seder;* even during the war when it was impossible to have a *seder,* you still whispered those words to yourself. Now, the dream is coming true. For 2,000 years, Jews have wanted to return to *Eretz Yisrael,* and you, you of all people, are going to fulfill the dream. You can hardly control yourself, knowing that there will be delays and problems, but that you will ultimately stand facing the Western Wall in Jerusalem.

You make your way to the little town of Fiuggi, along the eastern coast of Italy, where the *Jewish Brigade* has established a center. It is called "Merkaz Lagolah," Center for the *Diaspora,* but in reality it is a center to prepare people to go to the Promised Land from the *Diaspora.*

Because you are young and strong, you are selected to attempt illegal immigration, to run through the British blockade on a ship called the Fede. This illegal immigration, or *Aliyah Bet* as it is called, is considered vital if a Jewish state is to survive. Since everyone is convinced that the Arabs will attack as soon as independence is declared, you will be needed to protect the new country.

Finally, you stand in front of the holy Western Wall, the remaining section of the great Temple in Jerusalem. You approach the ancient stones and whisper a prayer of thanksgiving to God for having brought you through the Holocaust, allowing you to reach this holy place.

END

142

You travel to Toronto and settle in an area where many Holocaust survivors live. It is important to you to be able to communicate with others who have shared your experiences. It is as though you belong to a special, exclusive club, a club to which no others can ever belong.

You secure a modest job with the Toronto city government, inspecting restaurants for cleanliness and proper health standards. You are happy in your job because you are constantly meeting interesting people, especially among the many immigrant groups which have arrived in the city.

But the job is only a minor part of your new life. What really matters is being with your adopted "family" of survivors, talking with them after *Shabbat* morning services at the synagogue, eating with them at their homes or at restaurants, sharing their *simchas,* and helping them, as they help you, through difficult times. The most meaningful time for all of you is the communal commemoration of *Yom Hasho'ah* every spring, when you remember the martyrdom of European Jewry. You cry bitter tears over the loss of your family, but you thank God for those who did survive, and you spend as much time as possible teaching children about what happened during those terrible years.

END

143

It takes nearly all the money you have, but a bribe to the ticket seller at the railroad station in Szeged is your only chance. She gives you a ticket that will take you all the way across Hungary, changing trains in Budapest and ending up in the provincial capital of Gyor. "Once you are there, my Jewish friend," she says sarcastically, "you're on your own." However, you have little choice; Gyor is as far west as you can get in Hungary, your only opportunity to get out of Eastern Europe.

When you arrive in Gyor, you walk to the Szechenyi Ter, the central square of the town where you notice a strange tree stump, covered with iron plates and thousands of nails. A friendly passer-by stops and tells you that apprentices learning the iron trade used to put a nail in the stump to show that they had passed by.

"I feel like that stump myself," you comment, "after all that has happened to me during the war. Only I have no home, nowhere to pound in my own nail." The stranger takes you by the arm. "Come! I'll show you a place where you can feel completely at home."

He leads you to an apartment on Tanaczkoztarsasag Utja, a boulevard which leads through the town. Seated around a table, to your great astonishment and joy, are representatives of *Brichah*, the organization which helps Jews leave Eastern Europe. With great excitement, you receive a promise of help. It is only left for you to choose the route.

If you decide to go west through Bratislava,
turn to page 127.

If you choose to go south to Italy,
turn to page 92.

144

Being Jewish has cost you dearly. You've learned the bitter and painful lesson that to be a Jew can be dangerous, even fatal. In quiet moments, you are angry that your grandparents or parents did not leave Judaism and become Christians.

Perhaps Christianity is the solution to your problems. It could also be the answer to the world's problems. On the other hand, too many wrongs have been committed in the name of Christianity for you to believe that this is the way to peace and brotherhood.

Looking around, you find only one choice left. You join the Communist party, the party which has long preached ideals you find attractive: peace, truth, equality, sharing—things that are important to you. A job in a party office permits you to rise slowly through the ranks until you are a well-respected official.

One Simchat Torah, you see a crowd of Jews dancing outside the synagogue. Curious, you enter. Someone offers you a seat and hands you a prayer book and a *talit.* You read the words about Torah and about the covenant between God and the Jewish people. You feel a power within yourself, urging you to change your life.

You decide to become involved again in the life of the Jewish community and synagogue. When you abandoned your Judaism, you never realized how much you would miss being part of this life. Now you plunge in with renewed energy and enthusiasm. Every *Shabbat,* you sit in the synagogue, and you feel totally at home. Finally, you are at peace.

E N D

145

As part of your agricultural training, you have learned to grow wheat, and you approach your new responsibility with confidence. The town of Morden is not so far from Winnepeg that you feel isolated; in fact, you are able to get into Winnepeg for Saturday morning synagogue services at least once each month and, of course, for all the holy days. It feels good to *daven* sitting in the same *shul* as your cousin and his family, the only family you have left in the world.

However, one problem you had not anticipated on your new job was locusts. Immense swarms of these pests fly out of the American Rocky Mountains and sweep through the northern Great Plains and southern Canada. Your crops lie directly in their path, and the locusts do not spare them. When you walk across the fields, all you can find are bits and pieces of stubble. The owner of the wheat farm has lost everything, and you have lost your job.

After considering your position for a while, you decide to go to college and then on to law school. When you graduate, you open a law office in Winnepeg, devoting your efforts to protecting the interests of small farmers and store owners, building a reputation as the defender of the underdog. This choice does not make you as wealthy as other lawyers, but you are satisfied that you are doing something important with your life.

When your friends elect you president of the Winnepeg chapter of the Canadian Jewish Congress, you know that your efforts have been worthwhile. The honor paid to you by your friends is more important to you than any amount of money. You are a very happy person.

END

146

German officers are proud of the fine Swiss watches they wear on their wrists and insist they be kept in excellent repair. Your claim that you are a watchmaker gets you assigned to a small workshop where three other people work at repairing timepieces. You don't really know what you are doing, but the others help you out, and you learn quickly—fortunately for you because false claims to special skills are punished with a slow and painful death by hanging. Perhaps it is the skill with instruments that you learned in medical school that saves your life.

In November 1944, as the Russian army approaches Auschwitz from the east, the guards destroy the crematoria, shred the records which tell about the 1,500,000 people killed in the camp, and then try to flee the advancing enemy. As discipline in the camp breaks down, you escape.

You are afraid of ending up in Russian hands so you travel west to the German city of Mannheim. An American army chaplain tells you he knows nothing about watchmaking, but he offers you another possibility.

"When I arrived in Mannheim," he tells you, "I found the holy books from the Old Age Home buried safely in the garden behind the building. There's no place for them in Germany anymore; I am sending them to the library of the Hebrew Union College. If you would like to accompany them, you might find work. I could recommend you."

You accept the chaplain's offer and soon find yourself in Cincinnati, Ohio, sorting and cataloguing books. The people are kind and helpful, and you are happy to be alive. You decide that this is where you will spend the rest of your life.

END

147

With the help of the resistance and various other underground groups, you are finally able to reach the little town of Le Chambon. Le Chambon is an old settlement of French Huguenots, people who recall persecution they once experienced at the hands of French Catholics. Because they remember, they help others, Jews and non-Jews, escape from the Nazis. Along the way you have been hidden in hay lofts, wine cellars, and even tree tops in orchards. Farmers and their families have risked their lives to shelter and feed you because of a lack of sympathy for the Nazis.

Now, after hiding several more days in a cellar, a villager leads you and several other Jews into Switzerland. The journey is treacherous, especially at night, and you must be very careful. A great deal depends on the success of the trip; you arrive without accident. With the help of Swiss friends of the Chambonnais, you arrive in the Swiss city of Montreux.

You sit on the shore of Lake Geneva and gaze at the *Château de Chillon* where once another prisoner pondered his fate.

If you believe that you were a prisoner of the Nazis and are now free, turn to page 95.

If you feel imprisoned in the jail of Judaism, turn to page 30.

148

You must fight the Germans. After all they have done to the Jewish people, not to mention your own family, you feel compelled to take an active role in their defeat. To do less would be to put your own safety above the rescue of your brothers and sisters, and you cannot allow yourself to do that.

You are assigned to a resistance unit near Lyon, a unit composed mostly of Jewish young people. Together with Anny Letour and Jean-Pierre Levy, you attack German communications and transportation. It gives you special pleasure to rescue Jews from convoys before they can be deported to concentration camps. The "Organization Juive de Combat" (Jewish Fighting Organization) helps get some of these rescued Jews into Switzerland and Spain. You feel that you are doing something intensely important each time you save a single Jewish life—as though *you saved the entire world.*

Later, as it becomes clear that the Allied armies will land on the beaches of northern France, you and other members of the resistance move north and attack German installations near Calais. These diversions help convince Hitler that the landing will come there. When it actually occurs at Normandy as a surprise to the Germans, you feel that all the dangers you endured were worthwhile. Later, General Charles de Gaulle decorates you with the "Medaille Militaire." You settle in the town of Caen as a shopkeeper where you are respected by your neighbors and satisfied with yourself. What more could anyone ask?

END

149

You move in with the Savigny family. In their small apartment at the base of Montmartre, they make you feel welcome and comfortable. After a few months, you even think of yourself as the person whose identity you've assumed. You begin to venture out of the apartment, walking along the streets, stopping in sidewalk cafes, browsing in shops. Every morning, you spend a half-hour at the Basilica de Sacré-Coeur, learning from a friendly priest how to behave like a Catholic. Soon, you can attend mass without anyone suspecting that you were not born into the Catholic Church.

You were fortunate to have made this choice because Mother Marie's Convent of the Little Cloister is raided by the Germans, and everyone there is transported to Auschwitz. Recalling with deep gratitude how these good people helped you escape, you are especially saddened by their fate. However, you are relieved that you were not hiding among them.

When Paris is liberated during the summer of 1944, you join the Savigny family near the Arc de Triomphe, waving the Tricolor, the French flag, and singing the Marseillaise. You feel that you have crossed a line; you have become a Savigny, and you can never return to your old self again. You ask the family if they would consider adopting you, and Mme. Savigny bursts into tears. "I thought you would never ask," she blurts out. With the help of the priest, you make a formal conversion to Catholicism and remain in Paris as the devoted child of this kind and courageous French family.

END

150

Traveling in German-occupied France is not easy. A young person, even with the best of documents, is always suspect, and you are frequently stopped and interrogated. You constantly explain that you are a nurse, hired to care for elderly people at a nursing home in Cannes. You have a letter from the home (provided by Mother Marie) which looks authentic. Despite some frightening moments, you pass along, moving constantly away from Paris.

Distance from the center of the German forces is important because the farther you are away from Paris, the less intense are the searches for Jews. The Vichy government of Pierre Laval has not been interferring with the deportation of Jews to concentration camps, and the Germans are pleased. Therefore, there is less pressure on the average person to cooperate with anti-Semitic actions. It's not that the people love Jews; they privately hate the Nazis and their Vichy puppets. Anything they can do to hinder collaboration seems good to them.

It takes you eight days to travel from Paris to Vichy. Now, you must decide whether to continue toward the Riviera or to take some other path.

To learn what happens to you in Vichy France, turn to page 32.

151

Lyon is not one of the French cities dominated by the Germans. The Catholic Church, especially, has worked diligently to save many Jewish children. Cardinal Gerlier, the Archbishop of Lyon, and Pere Chaillet conspire to hide many Jews in Catholic orphanages, hospitals, convents, and even churches.

They arrange to place you in the country home of a woman whose husband was executed by the Nazis for sabotage. When you talk to his widow, you learn that her husband had been active in blowing up trains and bridges, disrupting the German supply system. She hates Germans and will protect you at any cost.

When France is liberated in the summer of 1944, this woman urges you to remain with her. You have grown very close, and she thinks of you as her own child. It is true that you have come to admire and respect her. However, at times, you get a strong urge to move on to a new life. Of course, you must make your own decision for your future. Perhaps you can build a life for yourself in the United States.

If you decide to remain with the widow in Lyon,
turn to page 110.

If you choose to leave reluctantly, hoping to get to the United States,
turn to page 128.

152

Some Jews hide in the forests of Correze, but you choose a cave near the town of Bergerac, above the Dordogne River, sharing it with several other Jews. You even try your hand at writing poetry, like another famous resident of Bergerac, Cyrano. Unfortunately, your verse is not of the quality of his, and you return your thoughts to the urgent matter of survival. Fortunately, the "Organization Juive de Combat" (Jewish Fighting Organization) has excellent spies who always alert you to a coming German raid. With the organization's help, you are able to leave the cave in time and scramble up the hill to new hiding places.

Having survived the war, you reflect upon your experience. Recognizing that you could not have managed without the help of many generous people, you decide to return this favor by working to help other refugees. You journey to Geneva, Switzerland, and find a job with the International Refugee Organization, part of the United Nations.

The rest of your life is spent trying to help refugees find new homes and settle into productive lives. You find this totally satisfying. It is as though you were trying to fulfill the Torah commandment in Leviticus 19:16: "Do not stand idle while your neighbor bleeds."

END

153

Going north, you are fortunate to make contact with the resistance which helps you travel up the coast of the Bay of Biscay. Eventually you reach the port city of Bordeaux. Following directions given you by the resistance, you make an appointment with Aristedes deSousa Mendes, the Portuguese consul in charge of commercial and diplomatic matters. Upon hearing from you that the business you must discuss with deSousa Mendes is urgent, the consul's secretary arranges for you to come that evening at nine o'clock. You think that this is a strange time for a meeting, but perhaps the consul just works long hours.

When you arrive, you discover the reason. The consul and his secretary take you into the back room. They had known all along that you would be coming; the resistance had alerted them. Both of them are pious Catholics; the massacre of European Jews violates every belief of their religious faith. They respond by providing false papers for Jews, protecting them and then "passing" them into Portugal.

Your tears of gratitude are mixed with tears of joy as you slip aboard a small ship in Bordeaux harbor. Tomorrow morning, you will be well on your way toward Lisbon and a brand new life. You have survived, thanks to the courage of these two wonderful people; you will never forget what they have done for you.

END

154

You nose around Lourdes for a few days, hiding whenever Vichy police patrols pass. Soon, you overhear a conversation that suggests that a particular dealer in religious objects is, in fact, a member of the resistance. With the greatest fear of your life, you go into the store. The dealer takes one look at you, grabs you by the coat, and drags you into the back room. "You took a great chance in coming here, 'mon vieux.' But we'll 'pass' you into Spain."

Since few people can make the pilgrimage to Lourdes during the war, the dealer has permission to take truckloads of holy water across the border into Spain. Because of these frequent trips, the border guards know the dealer and wave the truck through casually without inspection. On one trip, hidden deep among the cases of water, you are driven uneventfully into Spain. You are safe!

If you decide to get as far from Europe as possible and arrange for a boat ticket to Mexico,
turn to page 94.

If you choose to remain in Europe, learn a trade, and start working,
turn to page 96.

155

Padre Benedette puts you in touch with the mayor of a small town, Orsogna, who provides you with yet another new identity. You now appear to be a good Roman Catholic, born, baptized, and raised in that little place. Your new documents state that your mother was German, the explanation for your fluency in that language.

With your new documents, you go south toward the area where active combat is taking place. In the city of Ancona, you find work as an interpreter in German headquarters. As a spy, you learn only one piece of information, but it is one that really counts: The Germans will pull back tomorrow as British and American troops advance up the peninsula of Italy.

As the Germans retreat, you sneak away and hide. As the battle continues, you find yourself behind Allied lines. You journey to Bari, where you make contact with advance units of the *Jewish Brigade,* a Palestinian unit in the British army.

After the war, they help you make *aliyah.* Your experiences land you a job in a reception center, helping other immigrants settle in Israel. You enjoy this work and continue it for the rest of your life.

END

156

Having made contact with the Italian resistance, you are assigned to help Ada Sereni. Her husband, Enzo, had broadcast radio encouragement to the Jews and resistance members in Italy, but he was captured and eventually executed in Dachau. You help his widow to continue his work. Neither your German nor your *Yiddish* is of any help since Italian Jews speak neither language. You content yourself with carrying the equipment and grinding the handles of the portable generator while Mrs. Sereni makes the actual broadcasts.

When the war ends, you must decide where to start your life again. You can make *aliyah* and live in *Eretz Yisrael,* or you can find your place in the *Diaspora.*

*If you decide to become part of the new
Jewish state,
turn to page 141.*

*If you choose to stay in Italy, hoping to
improve the quality of Jewish life there,
turn to page 132.*

157

The kibbutz of Ein Harod lies in the eastern part of the fertile Jezreel Valley which runs across the southern edge of the Galilee. This region is one of Palestine's most successful agricultural districts. When you remember that you came ashore packed as "Agricultural Equipment," you laugh. "I must be at least as valuable as a plow or a shovel!"

Most of the settlers at Ein Harod are German Jews, many of whom have been there for quite a few years. In the early days, they had to clear swamps, remove rocks from the fields, and protect themselves from hostile Arabs. Later, with the help of Henrietta Szold, they were joined by many German-Jewish children brought out of Europe by *Youth Aliyah*. Now, their fields yield abundant crops, but they are still afraid that the Arabs will attack, particularly after the state declares its independence.

You join these longtime *Zionists*. You learn Hebrew; you learn to tend the vegetable gardens; you also learn how to shoot a rifle, which turns out to be a useful skill. During Israel's War of Independence, the kibbutz is attacked, but you manage to repel the invaders. People fight fiercely. This is the only home they can ever have; there is nowhere else for them to go, now that Hitler has ended the possibility of Jewish life in much of Europe.

After the War of Independence, you commit yourself to a life at Ein Harod. You are happy to be among Jews who work together and care so strongly for each other.

END

158

By the time you get off the ship in Haifa, you have made your decision. As a Jew and as a human being, you must do whatever you can to stop Hitler; you must find a way to fight the Nazis.

That way is provided by the *Haganah,* the *Yishuv*'s semi-secret military force. You learn that units from the *Haganah* will soon be organized into a brigade of the British army and sent to Europe to fight the Germans. A strong inner feeling makes you enlist.

In reality, the *Haganah* is not much of a military force when you join. You use wooden rifles instead of real ones, and the British won't let you train the way a real army should. They believe that a true Jewish military force would anger the Arabs, and the British are apparently more concerned with Arabs than with Jews. Still, it's better than nothing, and you are proud to be with a Jewish military group. "Havlagah," restraint, your commanders counsel, and you all practice patience impatiently.

In May 1948, when the State of Israel comes into being, the *Haganah* is ready. Arab attacks nearly crush the new country, but you push them back, and an uneasy armistice is finally arranged. You and your fellow soldiers have helped make the new state a reality. This must be the reason you survived, you conclude, and the army becomes your permanent career.

END

159

You are determined to stay and fight the prejudice in your own "back yard." The *KKK* is a small minority, but so were the Nazis in Germany in 1933. You are sure that you can rally other citizens of Collinsville and prevent the spread of prejudice through the community. You hold meetings in your home, talk about your experiences in Europe to anyone who will listen, and address the City Council. The local newspaper reports your crusade.

However, you are not sure you are having any effect. Some people call you a "Commie," and others simply won't have anything to do with you. One evening, you are awakened to find a large wooden cross burning on your lawn and a sign, "We'll Finish What Hitler Started." You are frightened and furious. Perhaps you have made a terrible mistake, assuming that there were many good and caring people in the city. You are depressed; maybe you've failed.

Some of your non-Jewish neighbors come over and ask you to go to church with their families the next Sunday. "We know you don't have a synagogue here, but perhaps you'll find comfort with us. Don't worry! We won't convert you."

You agree to go. What a surprise! During the sermon, the minister calls you up to the pulpit and tells you publicly that the congregation supports your work. You are among friends who have chosen to honor your efforts. All your work has been worthwhile, and you spend the rest of your life with great satisfaction and fulfillment as a respected citizen in that small, southern Illinois town.

END

160

You are horrified. How can it be that you have so misjudged your neighbors. They are bigots, prejudiced people who might someday turn on you. After all, while the *KKK* started as an anti-black organization, it is now anti-Jewish, anti-Catholic, and anti-foreign as well. You cannot stay. You sell your business and move to Chicago.

There, you go to work for the Jewish Community Relations Committee of the Jewish United Federation. There can be no other work so important for you as trying to combat anti-Semitism by helping other people understand who Jews are and what they care about. You plunge tirelessly and passionately into this mission—as though your life depended on it. In a sense, it really does.

When you retire, leaders from the Jewish community are joined by prominent non-Jews at a dinner paying tribute to you. You are very grateful for the honors bestowed upon you, but, as you tell them in your speech: "The job is far from over. It seems we always have lots of folks who like to hate other people. You and I still have a huge task to accomplish." Until you die, you continue your crusade, helping Chicago and other cities improve relations among their citizens.

END

161

You board a rusty, leaking ship in Trieste harbor. The Italian commandant of the port has been paid to allow the group to leave; more important, he has been sympathetic to the *Zionist* cause. In any event, there is no opposition as the ship steams from the harbor and sets a course for Haifa.

Unfortunately, a British spy observed your departure, and the troops of the British *Mandate* have been alerted. When you arrive, the ship is surrounded, and no one is allowed to embark. After a few days, everyone is transferred to another ship, the S.S. Patria. A British officer informs you that you will be taken to the island of Mauritius for the rest of the war. You and your friends are overcome with despair. Can it be that all your efforts will be rewarded by exile to an island in the Indian Ocean?

During the night, someone attaches a mine to the Patria; the ship explodes and sinks. Unfortunately, a number of Jewish refugees die. However, you manage to get ashore and are taken to the camp at Athlit. In a daring raid, Jewish commandos free you from the camp, and you join their forces. You cannot stand by idly while other Jews are being killed.

You find a place as a member of the *Irgun,* helping illegal immigrants enter the country and fighting the British. But you are captured, imprisoned at Acre, and convicted of terrorism. When you are taken to the scaffold, you turn to the British soldiers and exclaim: "At least I shall die with pride for what I have done."

END

162

You, the Schwarzes, and others are at sea for months before you reach Manila. To your surprise, you find a community of nearly 700 German-Jewish refugees. Rabbi Schwarz becomes the rabbi of the community. When the Japanese conquer the Philippines, the military governor of Manila authorizes Rabbi Schwarz to continue providing for the needs of the Jewish community. After all, most of its members are Germans, and Germany is an ally of Japan. Besides, there is no tradition of anti-Semitism in Japan. Conditions are difficult, but at least you know you have a chance to survive.

You do survive, mainly because of the good rabbi and his efforts. However, you see no future for Jews in this part of the world. You make your way to the United States and, inspired by Rabbi Schwarz, become a social worker. You commit yourself to working in Jewish community centers and helping young Jews plan for their own future.

END

163

At the Feldafing camp, conditions are terrible, not much better than in Dachau. The Allies had not expected to have the job of housing the pitiful survivors of the concentration camps, and they were unprepared. They try to clothe you in an old German army uniform. You refuse; you would rather be naked than wear that hated uniform. The food is totally inadequate, barely enough to survive. You are placed with others, non-Jews, sometimes even former Nazis who are masquerading as refugees to escape punishment from the Allies. As a Jew, you get no special consideration despite the fact that Hitler singled you out for especially bad treatment.

When General Dwight David Eisenhower visits the camp a few months later, he is appalled at conditions and orders an immediate improvement. Things begin to look up. You meet another survivor, marry six months later, and have a child. "Hitler took a million and a half of our children," you tell your friends, "and it's our obligation to replace them as soon as possible. Without them, we have no future."

Eventually, you resettle in Atlanta, Georgia. (You want no more cold weather; freezing in Dachau was enough for you.) As you drive to the community's *Yom Hasho'ah* services, you tell your family: "We are the 'She'erit Yashuv,' the remnant of Israel, who have returned to show the world that the Jewish people is eternal. That is our obligation—to those who died, to ourselves, to God. We must be Jews; we must survive."

E N D

164

When you get to the Windsheim camp, you find that some other young Jews have already organized a chapter of the *Zionist* group called "Betar." They are determined to become strong and never again to allow the world to persecute them or other Jews. Mostly, they want passionately to go to Palestine.

A representative from the Jewish Agency by the name of Yehudah Arazi meets with your group and tells you that it is possible to sneak you out of the camp, through Switzerland and Italy and across the Mediterranean into Palestine. It will be dangerous, he tells you, but everyone in the group agrees to go, no matter what the cost.

British army trucks pull up to the camp, and you climb aboard. Later, as the convoy rumbles through Italy, you discover that this is an entirely fake unit. The 462nd Transport Company looks like a British army unit, but it really belongs to the *Jewish Brigade* in Bari. They've painted trucks and acquired fake documents so that they can rescue Jews and bring them to Palestine.

Arazi was right; the trip is not easy. You must sneak right under the noses of the British soldiers guarding Haifa. But you succeed, and you are glad.

After the War of Independence, you enroll at the Technion, Israel's new science university, and train to become an engineer. You will become one of the builders of the new land.

END

165

The thought of returning to Poland, with all its terrible memories and current troubles for Jews, is simply too much for you to bear. From what you have heard via the grapevine, your family has perished in the death camps. There are no good reasons to go back.

So, continuing your march toward freedom, you first enter Austria. You leave the area of the hated death and labor camp at Mauthausen, making your way to the small town of Krimml in the British Occupied Zone. From there, you hike up a long Alpine valley known as the Windbachthal and cross through a mountain pass. The path is wide enough for only one person at a time; any misstep will mean a long fall and certain death. You are very careful, and you arrive safely in the northern Italian town of Prettau in the Valle Aurina. From there, you are more fortunate, as you find buses and trains that will take you southward to Rome.

When you arrive in the Eternal City of Rome, representatives of the *Jewish Agency* direct you to the Balboa Street Synagogue, where people like you are caring for over five hundred Jewish children. You gladly volunteer to help these orphans; for the first time in six or seven years, you feel that you are doing something worthwhile.

When the children leave for Israel, you accompany them. Your dream of becoming a physician has not dimmed, and you enroll at the Hebrew University to finish your training. When you graduate, you become a pediatrician, working with the children of immigrants in a clinic in Tel Aviv. Your work with the children in Italy and the completion of your medical training have combined to make you a successful doctor—and a happy person.

END

166

The most precious thing for any Jew is "mishpachah," the family, and that is the reason you are driven to return to Cracow. Possibly some member of your family has survived. You must exert every effort to locate even one such relative.

As you reach Katowice, you inquire among Polish people about Jews who might still be living. You are puzzled by their cold reception and their unwillingness to answer. Then, you understand. First, of course, is the old problem of Polish anti-Semitism, which still exists in the country; second, they are afraid that Jews will come back and claim their property, property which Poles have now taken as their own and which they do not want to surrender. You get no satisfaction; your quest has met a dead end.

Chief Rabbi Yitzhak Herzog of Palestine arrives one day to rescue Jewish children. The *Joint Distribution Committee* has heard of Jewish youngsters who had been hidden, by their now-murdered parents, in Polish homes. Rabbi Herzog is to collect them and take them to Palestine. Over five hundred children are gathered at an orphanage in Otwotck; many others will never be found. You are offered the job of guiding these youngsters to the Promised Land.

At your first *Pesach seder* in Israel, you gather the children around you as you recite "Vehigadtah levanecha . . . ," You shall tell your children. . . . You tell them how your parents recited the *Pesach* story to you when you were a young child; you tell them about the modern Pharaoh who killed your parents, who almost killed you, and whose Holocaust has led all of you to this land of Jewish life. Together, all of you recite a prayer of praise to God for the privilege of crossing out of slavery and into freedom.

END

167

From Dachau, you move toward the west, eventually reaching the Schwarzwald, a dense forest in southwest Germany. You travel mostly at night, stealing food from small farms. You spend your days in hiding. Reaching the Rhine River, you cross into France, to Strasbourg.

You remember from your history books that Strasbourg was the city where the first French Protestant church had been founded in 1538 by Huguenot refugees. These French Protestants had suffered persecution at the hands of the French Catholics, and you are hopeful that they might help other persecuted people, like the Jews, escape the Nazis.

After entering the city, you soon find yourself looking up at the front of the great cathedral, at a statue representing the Jewish people and its synagogue. The synagogue appears bowed in defeat. You promise yourself that this will never happen; you and other Jews will keep Judaism alive.

When you discover that it is still possible to send telegrams out of France, you communicate with a close friend who had left Europe for a city named Milwaukee in the United States of America. Your friend quickly arranges the necessary sponsorship affidavit, and you are able to take one of the last ships permitted to leave France for America.

You arrive in Milwaukee, learn English, and make a decision: "I am going to join the American army, fight against Hitler, and help save Jews in Europe." You participate in the landings on D-Day and later enter Germany. There, you help arrest Nazi war criminals, including some who tormented you years earlier. Shoving them into prison, you display your Star of David: Judaism has survived. You have kept your promise.

END

168

The British army uses the former concentration camp at Bergen-Belsen as a place to care for refugees, Jews and non-Jews. Many of the people there have suffered terribly during these last years, but you are still relatively healthy. You volunteer to help the British medical staff, which works around the clock, desperately trying to save lives. Some of the people are simply too weak; you watch hundreds of people die from Nazi brutality—after the liberation, after they are finally free.

Bergen-Belsen has become something of a Jewish "city." Thousands of Jews have been moved into the camp; they need an organization to help manage their affairs. A young Jew from Eastern Europe, Yosef Rosensaft, becomes mayor of Bergen-Belsen. Soon he begins to plan for people to leave the camp and undertake new, productive lives.

You are assigned to work alone in a warehouse where possessions stolen from Jews by the Nazis are sorted and then given to people who have survived. As you dig through the piles, you find a large wooden box. When you open its lid, you are astounded to see three Torah scrolls, neatly and carefully laid side-by-side. You close the lid and walk quickly out of the warehouse to the office where a representative of the *Vaad Hatsalah* is talking on the telephone. You grab the telephone out of his hand and pull him over to the warehouse. When he sees what you have found, you both sit down on a heap of clothing and begin to weep. In a voice choked with painful sobs, you say to him: "These Torahs teach a lesson. Long after all the Nazis are dead, God and Torah and Israel will be alive!"

END

169

From Shanghai you travel to Djakarta, the largest city in Indonesia. In this Dutch colony, you meet a number of people from Holland who convince you that you would be better off if you went back to Europe and settled in Amsterdam. One of them even arranges for you to work at his cousin's diamond cutting factory, learning a new trade. You accept his advice and his help and go to Amsterdam.

You spend two years as an apprentice in the diamond cutting factory and then pass the examination which allows you to have a full job of your own. The cousin is pleased with your work and wants you to continue. There is no reason why you should not stay since you have been well treated by him and by all the other people you have met in Holland.

In May 1948, however, the State of Israel declares its formal independence. You read every newspaper account you can find and spend hours listening to scratchy radio reports at the Jewish community center. Something inside you tells you that you must go to Israel and take advantage of the citizenship offered under the new *Law of Return.* You arrange passage on a ship to Haifa and leave the kind people of Holland for the uncertain future of Israel.

North of Haifa along the Mediterranean, you rent a small building. With the help of the Rothschild family in England and the DeBeers Consolidated Mines Ltd. of South Africa, you begin Israel's diamond industry. Because you remember the kindness of the *Sephardim* in Shanghai, you begin to train *Sephardi* immigrants to Israel to cut industrial quality diamonds. This is a way of repaying their *tsedakah* with your own. You make a success of your business. You are sure that you have done the right thing.

END

Glossary

Agudat Yisrael · Orthodox association founded in Europe in 1912. After World War II, its surviving members lived mainly in Israel and the United States. They actively helped survivors of the Holocaust leave Europe.

Aktion · German word for the roundup of Jews.

Aliyah · Hebrew word applying to immigration to Palestine which, after 1948, became Israel. Aliyah Bet was illegal immigration, especially during and after World War II. Youth Aliyah applied to the mass immigration of Jewish children for settlement in Palestine.

American Jewish Committee · Founded by German Jews in 1906 to protect Jewish rights. Believed, during the Holocaust period, that private, quiet negotiations would be more effective than public protest.

American Jewish Congress · Founded by Eastern European Jews in 1928 to protect Jewish rights. Approved of public protests against the Nazis.

Anti-Defamation League (of B'nai B'rith) · Founded in 1913 to promote understanding between religious groups and races and to protect Jewish rights.

Arrow Cross · The most extreme and anti-Semitic of the political movements in Hungary before and during World War II.

Aryan · Referring to a particular race which Adolf Hitler believed was superior and should, therefore, rule the world.

Bar/Bat Mitzvah · A Jew who becomes obligated to fulfill the commandments. Also the ceremony for boys and girls at age thirteen which signifies that they are now considered adults by the Jewish religion.

Bench Gomel · Hebrew phrase meaning to say a prayer of thanksgiving.

Brichah · Organization active during and after World War II to help Jews leave Europe and enter Palestine, often in defiance of British restrictions against Jewish immigration.

Brownshirts · Private army of Hitler's Nationalsocialistische Deutsche Arbeiterpartei (National Socialist German Workers' Party) who helped him gain power in 1933 and were then used to terrorize and eliminate any opponents.

Bundist · A member of a Jewish socialist organization.

Chalutz (Plural: Chalutzim) · Hebrew for a pioneer, especially one who settled in Palestine and helped turn the country from a rocky desert into a green and productive region.

Chasid (Plural: Chasidim; adjective: chasidic) · Very pious and observant Orthodox Jew who is a follower of Chasidism, a movement founded by the Baal Shem Tov (1699-1761). His religious leader is called a *Rebbe*.

Château de Chillon · Castle located near Montreux, Switzerland; also the setting for a poem written by George Noel Gordon, Lord Byron, telling about a prisoner in the château dungeon and his desire for freedom.

Choni Hame'aggel · Miracle worker who lived during the first century B.C.E. A story in the *Talmud* (Ta'anit 23a) tells that he planted a carob tree which would take seventy years to mature so that his grandson would have its fruit.

Codes · Books of Jewish law, compiled between approximately 900 and 1600.

Daven · The way Orthodox Jews chant prayers with a swaying motion.

Depression · The name given to the period of time between 1929 and 1939 when many people were poor; businesses failed; and, in Germany, angry feelings led to the election of Adolf Hitler who promised to improve the situation. He blamed Jews for all the troubles.

Diaspora · The scattering (dispersion) of Jews outside Palestine/Israel.

El Male Rachamim · A prayer for the eternal rest of someone who has died. Often paired with the "Kaddish," a prayer of praise for God.

Elijah Gaon (1720–1797) · Also known as the Vilna Gaon. A great spiritual and intellectual leader of Lithuanian Jews.

Eretz Yisrael · Hebrew for "Land of Israel."

"Final Solution" · Hitler's policy, adopted in 1941, of killing all the Jews in countries controlled by the *Third Reich.*

Gemara · The part of the *Talmud* compiled between 200 and 500 in Babylonia; a legal commentary on the Mishnah.

Gestapo (Geheime Staatspolizei) · [Nazi] Secret State Police.

Haganah · Jewish self-defense forces in Palestine which became the Israeli army after Israel gained independence in 1948.

Haman · In the biblical Book of Esther, the villain who tried to kill all the Jews of his time.

Handwriting on the Wall · Referring generally to the biblical Book of Daniel 5:5ff.; means an omen or foreshadowing of an unpleasant future.

Hashem · Hebrew for "the Name"; another way to refer to God.

Haskalah · After 1800, some Jews of Eastern Europe studied modern European culture and preferred it to traditional Jewish ways. This movement was known as the "Haskalah" (Enlightenment); one who joined it was known as a "Haskalnik."

Hasmoneans · Also known as *Maccabees* who fought for religious freedom (168–165 B.C.E.) and whose victory is now celebrated by the festival of Chanukah.

Havdalah · Service separating the end of *Shabbat* from the following week.

Hebrew Immigrant Aid Society (HIAS) · Begun in 1909, HIAS became the largest organization helping Jews leaving Europe for America.

IRGUN (Irgun Tzevai Leumi/National Military Organization) · An underground military force in Palestine which openly defied the British government by bringing in illegal immigrants and by performing acts of armed resistance. Became part of the Israeli army.

Jewish Agency for Palestine · International, non-governmental agency centered in Jerusalem which assists and encourages the development and settlement of *Eretz Yisrael.*

(American Jewish) Joint Distribution Committee (JDC) · Founded in 1914 to relieve the sufferings of European Jews after World War I, it performed the same function during and after World War II.

Jewish Brigade · A military unit within the British army composed of Jews from Palestine.

Judenrat · The Jewish governing council appointed by the Nazis to rule in areas occupied by the German army.

Kiddush Hashem · Hebrew for "sanctification of the divine name"; martyrdom, dying because of what you believe.

Ku Klux Klan · An organization of white Protestants determined to keep America free of the influence of blacks, Jews, Catholics, and foreigners. It flourished between 1920 and 1940, but it still exists.

Law of Return · Law passed by the Knesset (Israel's parliament) to guarantee entry, safety, and citizenship for any Jew into Israel.

Lechah Dodi · Hebrew for "Come, my beloved," the title and first two words of a hymn sung to welcome the *Shabbat.*

Long, Breckinridge · American assistant secretary of state who was the chief policymaker in matters concerning European refugees.

Ma'ariv · Daily evening religious service.

Maccabees · See *Hasmoneans.*

Machzor · Traditional prayer book for the High Holy Days of Rosh Hashanah and *Yom Kippur.*

Mandate · After World War I, Palestine was governed by the British under an agreement called a "mandate," granted by the League of Nations.

Maquis · French underground anti-Nazi fighters during World War II.

Minchah · Daily afternoon religious service.

Minyan · The minimum ten men required to conduct a traditional Jewish religious service.

Mitzvah (Plural: Mitzvot) · Hebrew for "commandment of God"; a good deed.

Nationalists · The government of mainland China under Chiang Kai-shek. In 1949, they were expelled by the Communists and today control only the island of Taiwan.

Niemoller, Pastor Martin · Protestant minister who was arrested by the Nazis. Before his death, he said that he had failed to protest the arrests of journalists, politicians, and Jews because he was not one of them and that, later, when the Nazis came for him, there was no one left to protest his arrest.

ORT (Organization for Rehabilitation through Training) · Founded in 1880 in Russia, ORT promotes vocational and agricultural education among Jews. Following World War II, it was very active helping survivors of the Holocaust make new lives for themselves.

Pale of Settlement · An area that today would include parts of western Russia, Poland, Hungary, Czechoslovakia, Roumania, and Bulgaria. By 1885, four million Jews had been forced to move into this area, and more were driven in later by anti-Semitic governments. Living conditions were terrible. The Pale of Settlement was legally abolished in 1917.

Pesach Seder · The religious service and meal celebrating Passover. Pesach is the Hebrew for "Passover," the holiday commemorating the Exodus from Egypt.

Pirke Avot · That section of the *Talmud* which describes proper conduct and stresses Torah study and observance of the commandments.

Rebbe · The religious leader of a *chasidic* group; he is also a rabbi.

Riegner, Gerhart · Representative of the World Jewish Congress in Geneva, Switzerland, who relayed a report in August 1942 accurately describing what the Germans were doing to exterminate Jews in occupied lands.

SA (Sturmabteilungen) · Storm Troopers.

SS (Schutzstaffel) · An elite group within the German army which was responsible for running the concentration camps and dealing with any "enemies" of the *Third Reich*. It was led by Heinrich Himmler.

Sephardim · Jews from Mediterranean countries or their descendants.

Shabbat · Hebrew for "Sabbath." Erev Shabbat means the evening beginning the Sabbath (Friday night).

Shema Yisrael · Hebrew for "Hear, O Israel," the first two words of Judaism's most important prayer (Deuteronomy 6:4).

Shul · Yiddish for "synagogue."

Simchas · Yiddish for "joys." (Hebrew: simchah, joy.)

Sonderkommandos · Squads of death camp inmates who were assigned to remove the corpses of those murdered by the Nazis. They were generally killed themselves to eliminate witnesses.

Talit · The fringed prayer shawl worn by traditional Jews. (See Numbers 15:38–39.)

Talmud · The Babylonian Talmud (about 500 C.E.) contains the Jewish laws of that period, legends, stories, and disputes and is considered more authoritative than the Palestinian or Jerusalem Talmud (about 450 C.E.). The Talmud still forms the basis for traditional Jewish practice.

Taught You How to Swim · According to the *Talmud* (Kiddushin 29a), a father is required to teach his child to swim.

Third Reich · Hitler's empire which was supposed to last 1,000 years but actually endured only from 1933–1945.

Tishah Be'av (Ninth of Av) · A solemn day of remembrance for the destroyed Temple in Jerusalem.

Tsedakah · Hebrew word for "righteousness"; charity.

Tsedek, Tsedek Tirdof · Hebrew for "Righteousness, righteousness shall you pursue " (Deuteronomy 16:20).

Umschlagplatz · German for a collection place. Usually a large area where Jews were brought together before being deported to the concentration camps.

Vaad Hatsalah · Hebrew term for "Council of Rescue." An Orthodox Jewish group that sent agents into Eastern Europe to assist Holocaust survivors.

Wise, Stephen S. (1874–1949) · Reform Jewish rabbi and *Zionist* leader; founder of the Jewish Institute of Religion. Active in American opposition to Hitler.

Yad Vashem · Hebrew for "a monument and a memorial" (Isaiah 56:5). Memorial in Jerusalem to the victims of the Holocaust.

Yeshivah (Plural: Yeshivot) · Hebrew word for a school for advanced study; a rabbinical academy.

Yiddish · A language which mixes medieval German, Hebrew, and Slavic words and which became the daily language of most European Jews.

Yishuv · Hebrew word for a "settlement." The Jewish community in Palestine before World War II.

Yom Hasho'ah · Hebrew for "Holocaust Memorial Day."

Yom Kippur · The Day of Atonement, one of the two High Holy Days, is the most solemn occasion of the Jewish calendar. It is a day of fasting and repentance.

You Saved the Entire World · The full quotation is "Only one person was created to teach that . . . if one saves a single life, Scripture considers that he has saved an entire world." (Mishnah, Sanhedrin 4:5).

Zionist · Person who supports a Jewish homeland in Palestine, either by donations or by moving there.